Borderland Noir

Stories & Essays of Love &
Death across the Rio Grande

EDITED BY CRAIG McDONALD

D1247713

BORDERLAND NOIR
Stories & Essays of Love & Death across the Rio Grande

First published in the English language worldwide
by Betimes Books 2015

www.betimesbooks.com

Cover design by JT Lindroos

ISBN 9780992967499

Last night the children were singing
They said God drew a line in the sand
And one side was milk and honey
The other was Mexican land
La Frontera they don't understand
That the border is an evil of man.
— Tom Russell, La Frontera

CONTENTS

Afterword

FOREWORD

"*Nobody cared if I died or went to El Paso.*"
Crime novelist Raymond Chandler tossed off that snappy line in *The High Window.*

Tom Russell, the brilliant songwriter, essayist and painter who's spent years living in El Paso — an artist in every sense and one who also holds a master's degree in criminology — excerpted that nugget of Ray's for the sleeve of *Borderland*, his album that inspired the theme of this collection and at least half its title.

James Crumley, the godfather of the flavor of crime fiction I most revere, also lifted the same line from Chandler as an epigraph for his novel, *The Mexican Tree Duck.*

Confluences, unexpected connections and serendipity. All roads lead to borderlines of one sort or another, eventually.

The troubled, uneasy heart of this collection began beating many moons ago, in the waning days of 2005. I had just completed drafts of two novels still years from publication. The first was *Head Games* (2007), my 1950s-era debut about an aging novelist named Hector Lassiter and his trials along the Mexican border after acquiring the long-missing skull of Pancho Villa.

The second was *El Gavilan* (2011), a novel about illegal immigration and its stresses on a small Ohio town. The first was written mostly from my imagination. *El Gavilan* was inspired by things I was seeing and covering as an Ohio journalist. In that latter novel I was writing what I was living, so to speak.

A few days after wrapping *El Gavilan*, I was invited by crime novelist Dave Zeltserman to guest-edit an edition of his distinguished but now long-gone e-zine, *Hardluck Stories*.

I impulsively pitched a theme of stories set along the border and sold Dave on going live with the collection on Cinco de Mayo, 2006. I dubbed the collection *Borderland Noir*, partly in tribute to Tom Russell's album, as well as the brand of fiction I figured I was writing at the time.

The term "borderland noir" has subsequently become many a publishers' marketing slogan and a slice of frequently-seen book reviewer shorthand for a certain flavor of dark fiction set along the border. I'm pretty sure Cormac McCarthy is the undeclared but universally accepted standard-bearer of this still-growing genre.

With Mr. Zeltersman's blessing, I wrote a solicitation for stories that was really a thinly disguised mission statement for my two unpublished novels.

It went like this:

"La frontera, what El Paso-based songwriter Tom Russell describes as 'that delicious, dark-eyed myth of the border.'

"We're headed way out west, out past where you've dared to go before. Out to *Touch of Evil* country (that's the film, not the book, hombres).

"Our troubadours are Russell, Dave Alvin, Marty Robbins and Ry Cooder. Mariachi bands dominate the shortwave radios down this way, where tortured widower Orson Welles hands out justice with his ham-sized fists, all the while muttering under his boxy Stetson.

"We're not looking to be slavish about the coordinates: The Border is a state of mind every bit as much as it is a geographic boundary. But fiction or nonfiction, we will be seeking that Malcolm Lowry/ Day of the Dead/Cinco de Mayo vibe.

"Focus on that uneasy friction between Old *Meh-hi-co* and *El Norte*, because, way down deep, we all know that you can leave Brownsville, but you can never get Matamoros out of your soul.

"Give me stories about young lives snuffed out chasing the dream of more money and better futures up north.

"Show me guilt-stricken coyotes who can no longer stand to roast peasants in locked freight cars, or to abandon babies and their too-young mothers in the scrub-oak purgatory of the Sonoran desert.

"Tell me tales of Narcotrafficante madmen with too much cash and bent imaginations who build crazy tunnels under miles of dusty wasteland to smuggle drugs. I'm craving stories about bad bastards who kidnap tourists and mail them back one-finger-at-a-time, seeking impossible-to-pay ransoms from gringo wage-slaves whose one foreign vacation has gone so terribly south on them.

"To this day, cherry boys with butterflies in their bellies steal across the border to get laid, to drink rum at TJ's infamous 'longest bar in the world' and to find out exactly what the hell a 'Donkey Show' is. But sometimes things take a turn. Rum and tequila and first sex are a treacherous mix. Show me how treacherous.

"Emiliano Zapata said, 'It's better to die on your feet than to live on your knees.' So, in that spirit, swing for the fences, amigos. Give me strong and original voices. Gut-shoot me and/or break my heart, because, tonight, I just want to *feel* something."

And so it went. The year, as I said, was 2005.

It's 2015 at this writing, and it's demoralizing how little has changed in a decade when it comes to turmoil not just along the U.S.-Mexican border, but along many other troubled but tantalizing frontiers where struggling populations butt up against more prosperous—or still more tragically— simply safer-seeming neighboring countries where sanctuary seems an unspoken (and often unoffered) promise. The prospect of greener, less deadly pastures is a risky yet decided-upon choice for increasing numbers of desperate immigrants across virtually every one of Earth's continents.

In 2014, it was estimated there were almost sixty million refugees and internally displaced people around the globe. That breaks down to about one in every one hundred and twenty two people in the world fleeing from some *here* to some *there*, it was determined.

So now it's time for *you* to wade into the troubled, roiling river coursing yonder.

Different peoples sometimes call the same body of water by different names.

It's the Rio Grande to us living north of the border. South of the border, that same river is known as the Rio Bravo. Perspective changes everything. Maybe riverbanks do, too...at least for some.

The collection of stories and essays that follows is a mix of the old and new, some of the first *Borderland Noir* pieces, stirred in with some fresher works that hew to the still lamentably relevant original's dark template.

I'm not going to sum up these pieces or characterize them in any way for you.

It's more potent to confront them as I did, without preparation and like some treacherous, suddenly stumbled across river of uncertain name and origin, coursing between that aforementioned here and there, which can, in the end, be *anywhere*.

The Tecate is ice cold and a storm is roiling across the desert. The rain's musky fragrance rides the blast-furnace wind as a jukebox grinds on in a cantina's corner: Freddy Fender crooning "Across the Borderline."

"A thousand footprints in the sand...reveal the secret no one can define."

But watch these writers try.

—Craig McDonald
2005 & 2015

THEN

Her grandmother was the first to die of thirst crossing the Sonoran Desert.

Holding her hand as the old woman passed, little Thalia looked off across the heat-shimmering sand and wondered again why they had left home.

Thalia's family went back seven generations in Veracruz where it was lushly tropical and sodden with rain. There, the Gómez family lived close by the Gulf Coast beaches— palm trees and fruit to pick and eat; the Atlantic Ocean, full of fish. At least, her mother said, they could never starve there.

Though they were getting along, they had no prospects for more.

After much arguing, the Gómez family set out for the distant border.

The further north they trekked, the uglier and emptier Mexico became for Thalia.

Her grandfather had been a Zapatista when he was only twelve. Consequently, Alfredo Gómez fancied himself more the vaquero than he had right to claim. Still, Alfredo had a plan. They invested a portion of their meager funds in two old horses and a mule. Alfredo loaded the mounts with jugs of water.

The unsuccessful crossers set out with too little water. That's what everyone always said. Alfredo meant to see his family well supplied for their border crossing. Thalia's grandfather set off a day's ride ahead of his family with the notion of depositing the water jugs at strategic points to see his family safely across the desert.

The money might have been better spent on professional *guias*. Thalia's father, Francisco, did meet with a couple of guides, what would now be called Coyotes, feigning interest in their services, but really only fishing for free tips.

Papa learned from the *guias* that they fed their clients, or "chickens," cocaine to make them walk longer distances…and to make them walk faster.

After buying the horses, Alfredo and son Francisco bought some white powder.

All of them, Thalia, her mother and father and four siblings; her aunt and uncle and two cousins and her grandparents, took the cocaine and set off on foot a day behind her grandfather, aiming for the distant Arizona border.

For the first two days, Thalia brought up the rear, walking backward, waving a tree branch across their dusty path to erase signs of their passage, anything that might tip the Border Patrol. The cocaine made the little girl approach her task with furious intensity.

Long after, Thalia would wonder if the cocaine hadn't been their undoing, clouding her father's and grandfather's minds from seeing the more sensible plan of her grandfather walking alongside them, keeping the mounts loaded down with water close at hand.

And she would later wonder if the drug-induced exhilaration had spurred her grandfather on to riding greater and greater distances out there alone and euphoric in the desert, the critical water jugs being dropped farther and farther apart by the old, wired Zapatista.

And if Alfredo was less the vaquero than he fancied himself, father Francisco was even less the guide.

A two-day crossing stretched into four.

They found less than a third of the water jugs left behind by Grandfather.

Sister turned against brother for want of water. Husband and brother-in-law were crazed by the blow and the thirst and out of their heads from the heat.

The two men came to a knife fight over a jug of water.

Their horrified, dizzy and drugged children looked on as they slashed at one another.

Thalia, only seven, sat with her grandmother as the old woman died from dehydration and heat exhaustion, her lips and tongue black. Her eyes were shrunken back into her head. Abuela's voice was a dry whisper. Sonya Gómez told her granddaughter, "You'll see it for me, Thalia. El Norte, it will be paradise. Your life there will be like a dream, darling."

They abandoned her abuela on the desert floor, already a mummy. They left Grandmother Sonya in the desert with Thalia's gutted uncle, then, days deeper into their death march, they left behind a cousin, a younger brother and Thalia's baby sister. The ground was too dry and hard to bury any of them.

When they reached the other side, it took two days to find Grandfather.

Alfredo at once set off with his horses and mule, headed back across the border to find and recover his wife's and grandchildren's bodies.

They never saw Grandfather again.

Chasing work and opportunity, the survivors of the Gómez clan kept drifting north across the decades. They became legalized citizens, picking fruit for stingy pay and cleaning hotel toilets and the houses of rich gringos.

Eventually they reached Ohio.

—Excerpt from *El Gavilan*
by Craig McDonald

PART I

NORTH OF THE BORDER

Hope, like an anchor,
is fixed on the unseen

COYOTE'S BALLAD
By
MIKE MACLEAN

"You'll blow your cojones off, if you no careful."

"Que?" asked Miguel. "You say something?"

The man behind the wheel adjusted his Stetson and flashed a third-world smile. His name was Cruz — no first name, just Cruz. "This road, she's a bouncy one," he said. "And you have that pistola in your lap. A good way to blow your balls off."

"You don't know nothing, loco," said Miguel. But he stowed his Browning under the bench anyway and let his gaze return to the window.

The U-haul rumbled along a rough gravel road, kicking up waves of dust. It was dark out, the sky thick and moonless. A good night to be a coyote. A perfect night, if it wasn't for the INS flood lamps, lighting up the desert.

Cruz yawned, puffing out his barrel chest. He made Miguel think of a bull stuffed in a flannel shirt. "So how many chickens we got back there?" Cruz asked.

"Ocho," Miguel spat, disgusted with the number. Just west of Agua Prieta, he'd guided ten pollos — six men, four women — over a trampled length of barbed wire into Arizona. For almost a kilometer, they snaked across the desert on their bellies, hiding from the Border Patrol's 4x4s. Somewhere along the way, two got lost. Miguel hated leaving them behind, but when he spotted Cruz waiting at the rendezvous, he knew the group couldn't linger. So he herded his cargo into the back of the truck and jumped into the cab.

Now, the U-haul was headed for the interstate. For Phoenix.

Cruz had a boom box on the dashboard, spinning bootleg CDs. The raspy voice of Chalino Sanchez rang out mournfully, juxtaposed with happy polka beats and tooting horns. The song was a narcocorrido, a Mexican drug ballad.

"*I know that they'd like to kill me,*" the boom box crooned in Spanish. "*But let me catch them sleeping, two or three I will take with me, with this .45, I will demand that respect.*"

Cruz drummed the steering wheel in time with the music. "Eight is okay. How much we charging? Nine hundred a head?"

Miguel nodded. "Sí, that's right."

"And we got ourselves a little bonus," Cruz said. He jerked his thumb at the back of the truck. "I saw that girl you brought in. Una chica bonita, even with dirt all in her face."

"She's only a child."

Cruz flashed his teeth again. "Not for long."

Miguel said nothing. He turned back to the window and peered out at the desert, trying hard to forget Cruz's crooked smile.

"*...first you must betray him,*" Chalino Sanchez sang from the boom box. "*...chest to chest I guarantee you, your hands will perspire.*"

Fifty miles outside of Phoenix, Miguel spotted a rest stop and said, "I need to piss."

"Sure, sure," said Cruz, pulling the U-haul over. "I'll stay with the chickens."

Miguel reached under the seat for the Browning and tucked it behind his back as he dropped out of the cab. There was a time when coyotes didn't carry guns. But that was before the smugglers organized into gangs, before the hijackings and the turf shootings. Now, Miguel went armed on every run.

The rest stop was graveyard quiet. Miguel took his time in the bathroom, splashing cold water on his face. In the mirror, his skin was sun-worn and wrinkled. Twenty-six-years-old, but looking forty. That's what being a coyote did to a man.

As a child, Miguel's family drifted the American highways like a feather on a quick running stream. They bent their backs in the fields. Picked citrus, lettuce, cotton. Always moving but never getting anywhere.

Back then, Miguel's home was the rear seat of a rusted-bucket Buick. He had no real possessions. Nothing to call his own but the clothes on his back and his sister's smiling eyes. Now, even that was gone.

He splashed himself again, the water bringing his thoughts back to the world. His watch said it was 2 a.m.

Almost time.

Leaving the bathroom, Miguel felt the weight of the Browning tucked in his waistband, touching his skin.

"Mierda!" Miguel cursed.

His heart pounded hard against his ribs. Cruz was gone.

Circling the truck, Miguel checked the cab again, thinking maybe the bastard was lying down across the bench seat. That would be just like him, taking a siesta in the middle of a run. But the cab was empty.

This can't be happening.

He pulled the Browning out and ran to the back of the truck, scanning the locks. That's when he spotted Cruz on the fringe of the parking lot, the big man stomping through some bushes, buttoning up his jeans.

Miguel jogged to meet him, the pistol low at his side. "Where'd you go?"

"Relax, amigo." Cruz bowed his head to put on his Stetson. "Just taking a leak."

"A leak, eh? Why didn't you use the bathroom?"

"Soy un ranchero. A farm boy from Sinaloa. I like giving the earth a little something to drink."

Miguel grit his teeth. He'd heard Cruz's voice crack, saw his brown skin go pale. *No,* thought Miguel. *Please, not this again.*

He marched to the edge of the lot, to the bushes Cruz had trudged out of. It didn't take long to find the girl.

She was sprawled across the hard desert floor, a few yards from the blacktop. Her skirt was torn. Her panties were around her ankles like a white flag of surrender. The soft flesh of her neck had gone black, squeezed by strong, rough hands. In Agua Prieta, the girl's eyes had reminded Miguel of his sister's, somehow filled with both sadness and joy at the same time. Now the girl's eyes were like dusty glass.

"Hijo de puta." Miguel's swear was a snake's hiss. But Cruz wasn't there to hear it. The big man was already heading for the truck, hands in his pockets. Slinking away like a guilty child.

"Why?" Miguel shouted, catching up to him. "Why'd you do this?"

Still walking, Cruz shrugged. "Lo siento. I'm sorry, Miguel. I don't know what came over me."

"Not good enough."

"Calm down," said Cruz, facing him now. "I'll pay you for her, okay? We'll still get plenty for the rest of them. I'll give you part of my cut when we get paid."

"No, you won't," said Miguel. And he brought the pistol up and fired.

The bullet caught Cruz high in the chest and spun him around. The big man stumbled, almost falling to his knees. Then he caught his balance and frantically ran for the truck.

Miguel stood his ground and pulled the trigger twice more — loud "pops" that broke the desert's silence. One shot nailed Cruz in the kidney. The other caught the back of the leg. The bullet passed through the kneecap, blowing out chunks of muscle and bone.

Cruz howled like a dying dog. He pitched forward, finally losing his stupid hat, and skidded face first across the blacktop.

By the time Miguel reached him, Cruz had rolled over to his back, desperately trying to draw a .38 from an ankle holster. But it was no use. Cruz couldn't make his body work. Too much blood had escaped.

Calmly, Miguel stood over him and squeezed one eye shut to take aim.

"No," Cruz pleaded. Blood and saliva bubbled from his lips. "You can't do this. Not over one little puta. There'll be a thousand more crossing over tomorrow."

Miguel shook his head. "I wish that was the reason. I wish this was for her. Maybe then God would forgive me."

The Browning bucked in Miguel's hand. Cruz's head jerked as the bullet punched out the back of his skull. Blood and gray matter followed in its wake, spraying the air with a red mist.

For a long time, Miguel stood there motionless, peering down at the slab of dead flesh that had been his partner. In his head, he could hear Chalino Sanchez again, singing narcocorridos. Songs of bloodshed and betrayal. As hard as he tried, Miguel could not shut them out.

The yellow Ryder finally rumbled into the lot, two minutes behind schedule. The truck belonged to the Santos brothers, rival Coyotes with fat wallets. Its reverse lights lit Miguel's face as it backed up towards him.

Miguel walked to the U-haul and unlocked the rear gate. One-by-one, the pollos hesitantly climbed out. Their faces were etched with fear and they clutched their possessions like a drowning man clutches a life preserver.

"Bienvenido a América," Miguel told them, as he opened the back of the Ryder. "Welcome to America. Now get in the other truck."

TO HAVE TO HOLD
By
KEN BRUEN

"I should have married Johnny Cash."
The cop was taken aback. Of all the things he expected her to say, this was never on the table.

He looked at her, the dishwater blond hair, the hard mouth, the slight, jagged scar along her cheek and the air of exhaustion she exuded. The coffee he'd sent out for was before her and she moved her manacled hands to take a sip, the Styrofoam cup tilted back, and he glimpsed very white teeth. He had her statement before him and if he could just get her to sign the goddamn thing, he might beat the gridlock, get home to supper before eight. His partner had gone for a leak and the tape recorder had been shut off.

She raised her hands, asked,

"Y'all could maybe take these off for a time?"

He could see where the metal had cut into her wrists and angry welts ran along the bone. He said,

"Now, Charlene, you know I gotta keep you cuffed 'til booking is done."

She sighed, then asked,

"Got a smoke?"

He had a pack of Kools in his suit pocket, for his wife, shook his head, said,

"No smoking in a Federal building, you know that."

She gave him a smile and it lit up her whole face, took twenty years right off her. She said,

"I won't tell if you don't."

And what the hell, he took out the pack and a battered Zippo. It had the logo, "First Airborne." He slid them across the table and she grabbed them, got one in her mouth, cranked the lighter, the smell of gasoline emanating like scarce comfort. She peered at the pack, Menthol, asked,

"What's with that, you're not a pillow-biter are you? Not that I have anything against Gays but I can read folk. I'd have you down for a ladies man."

He nearly smiled, thinking,

"Yeah, right."

In his crumpled suit, gray skin, sagging belly, he was a Don Juan. What was it his daughter would answer... *Not.*

She wasn't expecting an answer, said,

"Years back, I was working one of those fancy hotels, still living high on the hog, and I ran the bar. Guess who walked in, with his band?"

Her eyes shining at the memory, she continued,

"The Man in Black, he'd done a concert and they dropped in for a few quiet brews and some chicken wings."

Foley was impressed. He liked Cash, except for that prison crap he did, and in spite of himself, asked,

"No shit, the Man himself?"

She was nodding, the smoke like a halo around her head, said,

"I couldn't believe it, I never seen anyone famous, not, like, in real life. I gave 'em my best service, and in those days, I was hot, had some moves."

Foley nearly said,

"You still do."

But bit down and wondered where the hell his partner had got to. Probably gone for a bourbon, Shiner back. He'd return, smelling of mints, like that was a disguise. He asked,

"You talk to him, to Mr. Cash?"

"Not at first. I was getting them vittles, drinks, making sure they were comfortable and after, I dunno, an hour, Johnny said,

"Take a pew little lady, get a load off."

She rubbed here eyes, then.

"He had these amazing boots, all scuffed but, like, real expensive, snakeskin or something, and he used his boot to hook a chair, pull it up beside him."

She touched her face, self conscious, said,

"I didn't have the scar then, still had some dreams. Jesus."

Foley was a cop for fifteen years, eight with Homicide and he was, in his own cliché, *hard bitten*. There wasn't a story, a scam, an excuse, a smoke screen he hadn't heard and his view of human nature veered from cynical to incredulity. But something about this broad … a sense of, what…? He didn't want to concede it, but was it… dignity? A few months later, a Saturday night, his wedding anniversary, he'd taken his Lottie for clams and that white wine she loved. Had a few too many glasses himself—that shit crept up on you—and told Lottie about the feeling and Lottie had gotten that ice look. He wouldn't be having any lovemaking that night; she hissed,

"You had a shine for that… that trailer trash?"

His night had gone south.

And c'mon, he hadn't got a thing for Charlene, but something, her face now, in the middle of the Cash story, it got to him, she was saying,

"I sat down and Mr. Cash, he asked me my name, I done told him and he repeated it but with an S… like… *Shur… leen.* He had that voice, the gravel. Luckies and corn whiskey melt, give a girl the shivers, and then he said,

"That's a real *purty* name… how he said 'pretty.'"

She massaged her right wrist, the welt coming in red and inflamed. She said,

"I had me a leather thong on my wrist. My Mamma done give it to me, real fancy, little symbols of El Paso interwoven on there, and I dunno, I saw him look at it and maybe it was the heat, it was way up in them there nineties, even that time of the evening, and I took it off, said,

"Can I give you this?"

"His boys went quiet for a moment, the longnecks left untouched and them fellers could drink. He took it, tied it on his wrist, gave me that smile, sent goose bumps all down my spine, said,

"*Muchas gracias, senorita.*"

Then I noticed one of the guys give a start and I turned and June Carter came in, that bitch, full of wrath. Dame had a hard on so I got my ass in gear, got back behind the bar. They didn't stay long after, and Johnny never came to say goodbye, that cow had him bundled out of there like real urgent business. The manager, he come over to the bar, paid the tab and gave me one hundred dollars for my own self. What do you think of that, one hundred bucks, for like, real little service?"

Foley knew hookers. For fifteen minutes, they'd be lucky to get thirty and change. Charlene's face got ugly, a coldness from her eyes, mixed with… grief? She said,

"I was on a high, floating, my face burning, like I was some goddamn teenager, and not even that Carter cunt…"

The word was so unexpected and especially from a woman, that Foley physically moved back, re-considered the hand-cuffs. Charlene finished with,

"I was cleaning the table, them good ol' boys sure done a mess of wings and longnecks and there… in the middle of the table, sliced neatly in half, was my Mama's wrist band."

A silence took over the room, she fired up another Kool, taking long inhales like she was stabbing her body, her eyes but slits in her face and she said,

"When I'd be clearing up, I'd been humming, *I Walk the Line*."

Years after, Johnny came on the juke, the radio, that tune, Foley would have to turn it off.

Go figure.

When Foley's partner got back, minted almighty, his face with that bourbon glow, he brought some sodas and if he noticed the cuffs were off, he let it slide, turned on the tape recorder, asked,

"You grew up in El Paso, am I right?"

Charlene gave him a look, a blend of amusement and malice, said,

"Cinco de Mayo."

He looked at Foley, shrugged, and Charlene took a slug of the soda, grimaced, asked,

"No Dr. Pepper?"

Then,

"Damn straight, between Stanton and Kansas, you get to the bus station?... Turn right on Franklin, walk, like maybe a block-and-a-half?... Little side street there, we had us our place, me and my Mom, near the Gardner Hotel. That building is, like, eighty years old?"

Foley's partner gave a whistle, said,

"No shit?"

Like he could give a fuck.

Foley was pissed at him, felt the interview had gone downhill since he had joined them. Something like intimacy had been soiled, and he had to shake himself, get rid of those damn foolish notions. Charlene stared at him, asked,

"I know he's Foley. Who are you?"

"Darlin', I'm either your worst nightmare or your only hope, *comprende Chiquita?*"

She tasted the insult, the loaded use of the Spanish, then said,

"*No me besas mas, por favor!*"

He didn't get it, said,

"I don't get it."

She laughed, said,

"The next whore sits on your face, ask her."

He leant fast across the table, slapped her mouth, hard, and Foley, went,

"Jesus, Al."

His fingers left an outline on her cheek and she smiled. The week after, when Al asked his regular hooker for a translation, she told him,

"Please don't kiss me."

Foley wound back the tape, couldn't have the slap on there, then asked,

"So what brought you back to Houston?"

She shrugged, said,

"A guy, what else."

Foley looked at his notes, double-checked, then,

"That'd be the deceased, one Charles Newton?"

She lit up the cigarette she'd been toying with, blew a cloud of smoke at Al, said,

"Charlie, yeah, he promised me he'd marry me, and he was into me for Five Gs."

Al gave a nasty chuckle, more a cackle, asked,

"The matter with you broads, you give your dollars to any lowlife that says he'll marry you?"

She looked away, near whispered,

"He had a voice like Johnny Cash."

Al spread his hands in the universal gesture of *the fuck does that mean?* Charlene was thinking of her third day in Houston: one of those sudden rainstorms hit and she ducked into a building. Turned out it was a library and she looked to see if maybe they had a book on Johnny. Passing a Literature section, she saw a title... *To Have and Have Not.*

For some reason, she read it as *To Have and To Hold* and was about to open it when the librarian approached, a spinster in her severe fifties, demanded,

"Are you a member, Miss?"

A hiss riding point on the *Miss.* Charlene knew the type — the dried up bitter fruit of T.V. dinners and vicious cats. Charlene dropped the book, said,

"If you have anything to do with it, I'm so fucking out of here."

And was gone.

She'd have asked Foley about the book if Al wasn't there, but she shut it down. Charlie was the usual loser she'd always attracted, but he had an apartment near Rice University and she was running out of time, looks and patience. When she caught him going through her purse, she'd finally figured,

"What the hell?"

And knifed the bastard, in the neck. Then it felt so good, she stuck him a few more times… twenty five in all, or so they said. What, they counted? She was still holding the blade when the cops showed up and it was, as they say, a slam-dunk.

Foley said,

"You turned down the offer to have an attorney present."

She gave him what amounted to a tender smile, said,

"They'd assign some guy, and you know what? I'm sick to my gut of men."

Al was unrolling a stick of Juicy Fruit, popped it in his mouth, made some loud sucking noises, said,

"You're a lesbian, that it? Hate all men?"

She let out a breath, said,

"If I sign this, can I get some sleep, some chow?"

Foley passed over a pen, said,

"Have you some ribs, right away."

She signed and Al said,

"Now the bad news darlin'. Ol' Charles, he was the son of a real prominent shaker right here in Houston. Bet he didn't tell you that. You're going away for a long time."

She stretched, asked,

"And what makes you think I give a fuck?"

She got fifteen years. As she was being led down, Al leaned over, said,

"Come sundown, a bull dyke's gonna make you think of Johnny Cash in a whole new light."

She spat in his face.

Six months later, Foley went to see her. He didn't tell Al. When they brought her into the interview room, he was shocked by her appearance. Her frame had shrunk into itself and her eyes were hollow, but she managed a weak smile, said,

"Detective, what brings you out to see the gals?"

He was nervous, his hands awash with sweat, and he blamed the humidity, asked,

"They treating you okay?"

She laughed, said,

"Like one of their own."

He produced a pack of Kools and a book of matches. She looked at him, said,

"I quit."

He felt foolish, tried,

"You can use them for barter, maybe?"

She had a far away expression in her eyes, near whispered,

"They got nothing I want."

He had a hundred questions he wanted to ask, but couldn't think how to frame them and stared at the table. She reached over, touched his hand, said,

"Johnny was on T.V. last week, did a song called *Hurt*, he sang that for me."

Then she changed tack, said,

"You ever get to El Paso and want to cross the border, take the number 10 green trolley to The Santa Fe Bridge. Don't take The Border Jumper Trolley — it's, like, real expensive. Walk to the right side of The Stanton Bridge and it's twenty-five cents to cross and in El Paso, you want some action, go to The Far West Rodeo, on Airways Boulevard. They sometimes got live rodeo, and hey, get a few brews in, you might even try the mechanical bull, that's a riot."

Relieved to have something to talk about, he asked,

"You went there a lot?"

"Never, not one time. But I heard, you know?"

He looked at his watch and she said,

"Y'all better be getting on, I got to write me a letter to Johnny, let him know where I'm at."

Foley was standing and said,

"Charlene, he's dead. He died last week."

For a moment, she was stock still, then she emitted a howl of anguish that brought the guards running. She wailed,

"You fucking liar — he's not dead. He'll never be dead to me — how do you think I get through this hell?"

As he hurried down the cellblock, he could still hear her screams, his sweat rolling in rivulets, creasing his cheap suit even further.

As he got his car in "drive," he reached in his jacket, took out the packaged C.D. of Johnny's Greatest Hits ... slung it out the window, the disc rolling along the desert for a brief second, then coming to a stop near some sagebrush.

A rodent tearing at the paper exposed Cash's craggy face, and, viewed in a certain light, you'd think he was looking towards the prison.

Impossible to read his expression.

TRAILER DE FUEGO
By
GARNETT ELLIOTT

Starry night filtered through the lime trees. Tench leaned against a tailgate, his fifth cup of Jack and warm Coke in a steady hand, listening to his fellow corrections officers talk about the day's work. They hunkered in a circle a couple trucks down. Most were just off shift and still in their tan uniforms.

Someone came drifting over, the firefly glow of a cigarette cocked in his mouth. Tench smelled the sweat on him and frowned. It was Stewart, the new guy. Nervous. He walked up to the tailgate and stood there for a moment, shifting from one foot to the other while Tench stared at him.

"Shit, but it's hot," Stewart said at last. "Sun's been down a couple hours and it still feels like ninety."

"Probably is."

"Doesn't it drop at night?"

"Not much during the summer. You don't like heat, you shouldn't have moved to Arizona."

He let the implications of that hang.

Stewart pushed back strands of limp hair. "I heard you, ah, handled that situation for me today."

Tench grinned. Set his drink down and fished in his back pocket for a moment. Came up with a loaded sock and handed it over for Stewart to inspect.

"It's light," Stewart said, hefting the thing. A look crossed his face like maybe Tench was putting him on. "What's it filled with?"

"Soap shavings."

"Soap? What for?"

"Doesn't leave any marks that way."

"You actually hurt him with this?"

'Him' being Hector Tamayo, the little banger stashed in D Pod, where they put the violent types. Tamayo had threatened Stewart his first day on the job. Reached up through the cell bars and shoved something hard against his back. Whispered it was a shank and he could have Stewart any time he wanted, he didn't show proper respect. Stewart had told Tench and half the guys in the break room about it afterwards. Tearfully.

"Yeah, I hurt him," Tench said. "Took a couple swipes to the gut. Tough beaner, but he went down. He didn't have no shank in there, by the way. He threatened you with a piece of cardboard."

Stewart still didn't look convinced. About the sock, anyway. He kept lifting it up like he couldn't believe how light it was.

Tench grunted. Snatched the sock out of his hand. Swung, letting his wrist go loose at the right moment, so the weighted end hit with the proper snap. He caught Stewart on the thigh. The little soap chips made a crunching sound that echoed through the groves and Stewart went down on one knee, moaning. The cigarette dropped from his lips.

"S'all in the wrist," Tench said. "Pussy."

He chuckled. There was a smattering of laughter from the other officers. Stewart looked up at him with moist eyes.

"I didn't hurt Tamayo to protect you," Tench said. "I did it to protect the rep. Our rep. Guys like you are dangerous. Get hard, fast, or get out of jailhouse work."

Silence from Stewart. The other officers had gone quiet, too. No one was going to offer any objections. Not to Tench. He held the line against all the hard-asses in County, dispensing pain and intimidation where needed. Somebody had to. He made the job easier for the rest of the guards and they knew it.

Stewart wobbled to his feet, face downcast. Nobody tried to help him. He limped out of sight and about a minute later came the sound of a truck door opening, an engine turning over.

Conversation seeped back after the truck drove away. Tench finished his drink. He congratulated himself on doing a smooth job with Stewart. Old Tench, holding court from the back of his pickup. The other officers would come to him later in the evening, respectful, ask for a few pointers in handling cons. And he'd dispense wisdom based on his fifteen years working penal institutions from the deep dark South to Texas to this chicken-shit border town.

Someone was walking up right now, as a matter of fact. A tall silhouette in a cowboy hat. Tench felt his gut hitch with recognition. *Him?* Coming all the way out here? But that's who it was, Don Gustavo, a big smile plastered on his greaser face. Looking more like some old vaquero than the local head of the Mexican Mafia.

He took the cowboy hat off, held it over his chest. Tench started to say something but Gustavo raised his hand. "I know, you're uncomfortable talking to me here." There was some urgency in his voice. "I would like to have arranged a meeting, but—"

"Don't sweat it," Tench said, belching carbonation into the warm night air. "None of these guys are going to give a shit. But let's go around to the other side of the truck, okay?" No sense airing his dirty business where co-workers could hear.

They walked deeper into the lime's shadow. Gustavo looked pretty sharp for a greaser, Tench had to admit, with his neatly creased Wranglers and snakeskin boots. Had a nice belt-buckle on him, too; Navajo silver and turquoise, gleaming in the dimness.

"I brought you something," Gustavo said. He reached under his shirt and handed Tench a tiny package wrapped in duct tape, slick with belly-sweat.

"Whoa," Tench said, palming the bundle instantly. He knew what it was.

"That hasn't been cut yet. It came all the way from Peru."

Tench frowned. "You want me to distribute?" Not his usual kind of work with Gustavo.

"No. It's payment. I need you to do something, tonight."

Tench felt a grin creep around the corners of his mouth. He was holding about four thousand dollars' worth of blow, easy. And he knew a truck stop in the foothills where he could move it all in one night.

"There is a gentleman living in Dateland," Gustavo said. "Alone. He's had connections with *La Familia* in the past. I need some names from him and a guarantee of silence afterwards. I don't want him hurt badly."

"Not too badly," Tench said, still grinning.

"Observe some restraint, please. I may need him again."

"Okay."

Gustavo leaned close and whispered details: the man's name, an address in Dateland. Specifics about the information he wanted. Was there much security? No, the man did not have a bodyguard. No dogs. Probably owned a gun, so some caution would be necessary. Tench told him everyone in Dateland was armed to the teeth, so no worries. They shook.

"Something wrong, chief?" Tench said. "I've never seen you rushed before."

Gustavo's eyes narrowed. It was like twin cracks opening in his head, letting Tench see the cold fire that always burned back there. "Just do this tonight," he said. He put his hat back on and strolled away quick as he came. Tench flipped him off behind his back. Fucking Mexicans. Getting all uppity like they were serious mobsters. Like they knew half the crap they were talking about. He'd take their money, sure, but he was getting tired of second-generation wetbacks telling him what to do.

Then he remembered Hector Tamayo. The little greaser's cries echoing up and down D Pod, falling on ears suddenly gone deaf. And his smile came back.

He left the grove at midnight, where the party was still going strong. Some of the crazy fucks would be clocking back in at five in the morning, wouldn't even go home or change their uniforms. Tench had been there once.

A patrol car pulled up the dirt road just as he was pulling out and flashed its lights. He slowed, rolled down the window. The two young patrolmen didn't recognize his face, so he took the badge off his pocket and showed them that.

"Just having a party back there, officers," he said, pointing at the dark trees. "Just a bunch of screws cutting loose."

They laughed at that and waved him on.

He pulled off from the frontage road on the way home. Gave old Gustavo's stuff an experimental toot and hell yes, it was pure. Live current coursed through his teeth.

All the lights were on in the double-wide as he parked. Leeza was awake. Shit. Well, this was a working night and she'd have to deal. He winced walking up the steps and hearing her techno pop playing on the stereo. "Workout music," she called it. Leeza was from West L.A. and bitches up there obviously didn't know any better.

She was waiting for him at the kitchen table, scowling, cigarette in hand and a whole ashtray crowded with butts. Wearing one of his Sturgis T-shirts—goddamn it, the one with the Old English lettering. And a pink thong. Probably thought it made her look sexy, but all it was doing was reminding him the trailer's carpets needed cleaning.

"You're late," she said, like they were married or something.

"The fuck it is to you?"

She started screeching. He ignored her and rummaged in the refrigerator. Jesus, Leeza could screech. He'd picked her up two weeks ago at the Tapper, one of the skuzziest topless joints this side of Sonora, and he'd been stone drunk when it happened. He didn't remember sleeping with her. He wasn't sure he actually *had*, but she'd wasted no time moving her skinny ass and all her stuff into his trailer.

"You don't like it here," he said around a mouthful of cottage cheese, "you can get the—"

"Tench, honey?" Her voice had suddenly changed. She was looking at his eyes.

"What?"

"Are you tweaking?"

"What do you mean, am I 'tweaking'?"

"Did you score some…cocaine?"

She spoke the last word with reverence. Her sallow tongue slipped out and wet her lips.

"Maybe," he said, taking a step back.

Her face brightened like a vampire's. "You're holding."

"Calm down."

She came at him with crooked fingers, clawing at his jeans and belt buckle. He wasn't sure if she was trying to get the coke off him or give him a blowjob so he'd share. Either way was scary. He shoved her back and she collided with the kitchen table, spilling cigarette butts and a wave of ash.

"I said, calm the fuck down!"

But she sprang up, grinning. Started clawing for him again. He couldn't do this, waltz around all night with a job waiting for him in Dateland. He made a fist and clocked her as she groped for his pants, scarred knuckles connecting with her temple. She staggered into the little cabinet by the sink that held his shot glass collection. Both Leeza and the cabinet struck the linoleum at the same time. Glass tinkled.

Oh shit.

He bent to examine the collection. His Harley Commemorative had shattered, and there was a fracture in the little cup he'd won that night he sang karaoke at Gentleman's Choice.

Leeza made gurgling noises. He turned to stare pure hatred at the little coke-whore bitch. He could tell she was unconscious by the way she was breathing. Well, it was better than she deserved. He picked the cabinet up and carefully set it on the table.

In the bedroom he changed into coveralls, transferring Don Gustavo's payment to his bib pocket. No point trying to hide the stuff here. Leeza, when she came to, would tear the trailer apart trying to find it. He felt around under the bed and hauled out his old axe-handle, a worn leather gag, and a handful of zip ties. Nothing fancy for tonight. Gustavo wanted a quick job, and besides, Tench had learned long ago that his hands were his best tools.

He checked Leeza's breathing one last time to make sure he wouldn't be coming back to a corpse. The techno pop noise had faded but he busted up the stereo anyways, on account that it was hers and the loss of property would strike a karmic balance for his broken shot glasses.

And just maybe the bitch would get it in her head to leave.

He drove the pickup through the rock gullies of Telegraph Pass, desert night and the buzz of AM radio his only companions. Beyond the mountains the land stretched out in a gray blanket. It would take an hour of chewing highway to make Dateland, so he leaned back and drowsed a little, letting his hands and his eyes do the driving.

Hell, everybody wanted a piece of Old Tench tonight. The spat with Leeza aside, things were looking peachy. He had a uniform and he had mob connections and he could flit between both worlds like all those illegals slipping across the border. Four thousand dollars' worth of blow didn't hurt his self-esteem, either. He could make a down on a righteous truck with that kind of money.

Some weak-minded type might call him a torturer, might spit when they said the word, but the truth was there would always be a calling for someone who could ask questions and get answers. Someone who wouldn't balk when the screaming started. Was it his fault he was good at it? He'd read some-where that even certain bad-ass Nazis had had their limits, had broken under the strain of inflicting misery on other humans. Well, that wasn't him. Maybe an upbringing in rural Missis-sippi and a dad who dealt justice with a cattle prod would've set those SS fuckers straight.

He thought about that, and when the high beams hit the sign that said thirty miles to Dateland he slowed a little. Best to keep his mind on tonight's job. The coldness he'd glimpsed in Don Gustavo reminded him that the man, greaser or not, was someone you didn't want to cross.

He found the whispered address down a dirt road, about three miles from town proper. 'Town' for Dateland meant a Chevron with a convenience store attached, plus the rows of palm groves that gave the place its name.

His victim lived in a lonely double-wide. It kind of reminded Tench of his own place, only shabbier, surrounded by scrub grass and mesquite. He drove by it to check the num-bers on the dented mailbox and make sure. A light burned in the rearmost window. There was an El Camino parked on one side.

He continued driving past for about two minutes, cut the lights, then swung around and stopped. He'd hoof it from here. Place like this, you could hear things coming for miles around.

He hopped a drooping barbed wire fence. The moon was up and cast silver on a field of yucca and broken beer bottles.

His feet crunched glass as he walked. He could see the trailer's single lit window in the distance, winking at him, drawing him like the proverbial moth.

He'd heard stories about the people in Dateland. Not so much a place to live as a place to lay low. Criminals with warrants on them in other states, crazy old vets who strung claymore mines around their property. Of course, if the place wasn't dangerous, then Gustavo wouldn't have sent someone like Old Tench, would he? Would've sent one of his own soft greasers instead.

The trailer window drew closer. He stopped about forty feet away. His victim's name was Juan Smith, which sounded bogus and probably was. What mattered was that Smith knew some of the people hauling Mexican Sudafed across the border for meth kitchens in Southern Arizona. And Don Gustavo wanted to know who these people were.

At twenty feet Tench stopped again, listening. No sounds from the trailer. No sounds from the road. He was being too cautious. Gustavo had told him the man had no muscle around. He had to get this sneaking stuff over with quick, so he could start the real work.

He crept up to the window. Craned his head. The light was coming from a lamp and a black and white TV. There was a recliner propped in front of the set, and the back of a gray-haired head sticking above the recliner. He heard snores over the soft TV voices.

Cake. Fucking cake. He ran to the side door. Flimsy lock; he slid his pocket-knife into the jam and pried the bar up with a faint pop. Crept into a narrow hallway. Ahead lay the living room, TV and recliner. Juan Smith, snoring louder now. He'd get his wakeup soon. Tench hefted the axe-handle and grabbed a zip-tie out of his pocket. A quick blow to stun, not too hard. Then the zip-tie. Then the gag, until he was ready to talk.

Someone coughed.

Tench froze. The coughing sound had not come from the recliner. Where?

And now the gray-haired man was stirring, straightening up in the chair. Turning around to face Tench. It was Don Gustavo. He still wore the creased Wranglers and boots, but the cowboy hat was gone. The lips under his moustache curled.

"What're you doing here?" Tench said. "Where's Juan Smith?"

"Relax."

"What's going on?"

Gustavo settled his arms across his chest. "Do you have a gun?"

"No. You said—"

A tall closet next to the recliner rattled and the door slid back. A man stepped out. He had to stoop to clear the frame; about six-four, dark-skinned, heavy-shouldered, with a greaser haircut and an aquiline nose that hinted at Yaqui heritage. The man wasn't carrying weapons and didn't need to. Tench's fingers dug into the axe-handle.

"There are complications," Don Gustavo said, "in working both sides of the law as you do." His voice sounded far away, though in fact he had taken a couple steps closer to speak. His eyes were half-lidded. He nodded at Tench.

The tall dark man came forward. His face had the fixed expression of someone expecting violence. Tench cocked the axe-handle back, ready to swing but balking when he saw all that muscle ripple towards him. He swung. The heavy's hand flashed out and caught him at the wrist with fingers made of cinderblock. Tench balled his left and drove it into the man's stomach. More cinderblock.

"Go easy, Chuy," Gustavo said.

But the heavy was already tightening his grip, fingers closing on Tench's wrist with inexorable force. Plans flashed through his mind, desperate. Knee the guy in the nuts. Kick his shin. Lean close and head butt him. A thousand tricks he'd learned while inside. But pain and panic kept him still. His fingers were going numb.

"You beat a man yesterday, in that jail," Gustavo said. "Brutally. I understand this was done as a matter of principle. I can respect such a thing. I hope you can, too."

Tench shook his head, not understanding. Too much pain to make the connection.

"Hector Tamayo is my Godson," Gustavo said.

Tench heard the first of a series of pops from his wrist. The axe-handle clanked against the floor. He swayed and felt like he was going to pass out, but the heavy jerked him upright. Tench looked into his eyes for signs of mercy. No dice. There were blue-black lines on the man's corded neck that ran down to the top part of his chest, swirling together to form the portrait of a saint. Tench recognized the technique and dropped his head. Prison tattoos.

"Now, Chuy," Gustavo said, his voice almost a whisper.

The broke nearly every bone he had and left him out by the freeway. Trucks roared by until the sun came up. Someone must've finally called 911, because suddenly paramedics were swarming all over him, shaking their heads. He'd gone so limp they had to scrape the stretcher under him to get his body off the ground.

At the hospital a toxicology screen found cocaine in his system, and one of the EMT's had come across Gustavo's "payment" while the coveralls were being cut away. They had left that for him after all. A parting gift. The possession was dutifully reported and Tench got his pre-trial notice while still learning to spoon applesauce to his swollen lips.

He should've left the stuff at home, with Leeza.

Later, sitting upright in bed, he tried to think of a single prison in the Southwest where he hadn't worked and the cons didn't know him by name.

TUMBLED

By

STEPHEN D. ROGERS

Vinny stopped wiping the back of his neck long enough to gawk. "The hell is that?"

"A tumbleweed." Ray slammed the trunk closed.

"You mean they just roll around like in a fucking movie?"

"That's how they get their name. You ready?"

"I am if your AC works."

"It works."

The men parted and walked around to their separate sides of the car.

Over the roof, Vinny watched the heat waves rise. "How do you stand these temperatures?"

"The sun bleaches money from the dust." Ray climbed into the car, started the engine, and turned on the air conditioning. "I like money."

Inside, Vinny stretched to switch the fan to high before closing his door. "Money's why I'm here too, but I'm leaving as soon as we finish the job. You, on the other hand, choose to live in his shithole."

"So long as the money don't dry up, I do." Ray bounced the car over the curb and onto the road that led to a road that led to a road that led to a road.

Vinny shook his head as he stared out the window at the nothingness. "How can you stand the monotony?"

"I entertain guests."

Vinny snorted. "Some entertainment. A bottle of no-name tequila in a motel room where I had to press my face against the AC to feel anything."

"Just wait until you get your hands on the money."

"What if it's not there?"

"So long as drugs come north, money goes south."

Vinny held his palm up to the vent. He'd come south because his partner back home had heard about this thing, a way for Vinny to get out from under his gambling debts. "And how is it you figure the two of us are enough to convince them to give up the money?"

"They're expecting an ambush. They're not expecting to get killed."

"Okay then." Vinny glanced at the radio. Thought better of it. "You said you've done this before."

"This is number seven."

"So why won't they be waiting for us?"

"Seven is nothing compared to how many buys go down every single day, all along the border. The people up top don't even notice what I take. As to the people on the bottom, they're lining up to step into the dead men's shoes."

"Still, nobody likes losing money. How is it they haven't tracked you down?"

"You worried?" Ray asked the question as if to answer in the affirmative meant weakness.

"The thought had crossed my mind. Maybe this time they'll be ready."

"They won't. Preparation is not their strong suit. Easy money, that's what they want."

"There's nothing wrong with easy money."

Ray slowed to turn left. "There's no such thing as easy money. The more you prepare, the easier it seems, but money never comes easy."

"Lucky for us, you're the King of Preparation."

"That's right."

Vinny examined the desolation. "So why did you put out feelers? You can't tell me there's not one gun for hire in the whole wide state of Texas."

"If I use local talent, I risk someone talking where he might be overheard by the wrong people. These people, they think going to New England requires a passport."

Ray drove in silence. Vinny rode in silence.

The road allowed them to chew up the miles.

Vinny broke the silence. "So what happened to the guy who did the last job with you?"

"What do you mean?"

"You said this was number seven. Why aren't you using the guy who was with you on number six?"

"He wasn't available."

"Even for this much money?"

"Even for this much money."

"He the same guy that was in for the other five jobs?"

Ray shook his head. "I like to mix things up. Helps with the monotony."

"I'd go crazy living here."

"Some people do. The craziest ones, they go up north."

"Huh."

Vinny had never been to Texas before, and he didn't see himself rushing back anytime soon, not even for another job that paid as well as this one. The place just didn't seem natural.

Tumbleweeds. Who would have believed tumbleweeds actually existed?

And that you could drive through so many miles of flat oblivion? Drive as though headed for the end of the world?

Vinny checked his watch. This was Ray's plan, all the way, and if in fact Ray had already done this six times without getting caught, he knew what he was doing. The question was: what wasn't he saying?

"So how do you keep the cops off your back?"

"Smoke and mirrors, my friend. Smoke and mirrors."

An answer that was no answer. Unless it was the answer. Maybe Ray had created an illusion that led them astray.

An illusion such as what? A drug deal gone bad, both sides killing the other? The guns would tell a different story. Not to mention the lack of product or money.

How did Ray convince everybody to look elsewhere? How did he convince them to not to focus on him?

Ray slowed to take the next left.

Didn't quite slow enough, and Vinny felt himself pressed against the door.

You convinced people the job wasn't done by a local by giving them reason to believe outsiders were responsible. Northerners, sweeping in for the easy money, and then flying out afterwards.

The desk clerk at the motel might remember the stranger who talked funny, but that didn't quite seem enough to misdirect an investigation.

And while he was flying under his own name, why would investigators focus on him out of all the people who flew in and out of Texas? And if they did, and had in the past, that meant Ray was depending on his guest to remain silent.

The whole thing just didn't make sense.

Unless Ray knew his guest wouldn't say a word.

Unless Vinny's partner felt like downsizing.

Unless Vinny would be discovered at the scene, his body pointing north.

Then it would work.

Vinny studied the empty wilderness as Ray kept his foot on the gas.

The dust rose behind them, joining the earth and the sky.

READING THE FOOTNOTES
By
JOHN STICKNEY

My partner and I are sitting in a light tan Pacifica, kind of blends in with the desert dust surroundings. AC set on high and we need it. The outside weather is scorching and the inside weather, well we are listening to Bob Marley's "Africa: The Singles" because it is my day to program the music. This music is hot, too. Not desert hot, Caribbean ganja hot. No surprise, you expect it to be hot inside and out when you're looking for the Devil.

In our line of work, we spend a lot of time in cars, driving somewhere to determine what has to be done. We act, then, receive orders to drive somewhere else, and repeat the process. We spend *a lot* of time in cars.

You know how it is when you're in a car and in your head you want to hear something, but the guy in control of the radio is playing something entirely different? Like being a teenager again, sandwiched into the back seat of your father's station wagon on a family vacation, driving to an isolated cottage on some small lake for a week of mosquito bites and fish nibbles, spending the ten, twelve, fifteen travel hours listening to the music of his, not your, life. Unless Dad is a fan of thrash metal or Emo or new wave or whateverthefuckteenagerslistentothesedays, you spend your time sitting in the back seat willing yourself to go deaf. Wishing, praying, "Make me deaf, God, please." I had enough of that shit growing up. So, two months into our partnership I told my partner, to whose musical tastes I have been deferring because of his one year and six-months of seniority on the job, I told him I am not your teenage son and I get to control the radio some of the time. He could tell I felt strongly about it, 'cause we're partners.

"Damn man, you shoulda said something." He pointed to the radio dial, as if to say, have at it.

This was not our first serious partner-to-partner discussion. There are other things I feel passionate about. For example, two weeks into our partnership, our first serious discussion went like this:

"Just so you know," I told him, "I do not kill children."

"Moral thing?" he asked.

"It's difficult to quantify," I said.

"No problem," he said. "I'm the same way about red-heads."

"Male and female?"

"Just female. Something to do with my first girl friend I guess."

I know, in comparison my love of music seems trivial. But I really love music, all types, all kinds, as long as it is good. Since we're good partners, we've compromised. If called for, he'll be the one to do the kill I won't, I'll do the one he can't and we both get to control the radio/ tape/ CD/ MP3/ iPod player on an alternating 24-hour basis.

When it's my partner's turn to program, we listen to classic rock, lots of Tull and EL&P and Floyd and Zepplin (he says he got the taste for that retro stuff from his parent's vinyl collection). Sometimes we'll listen to that political talk radio crap or sports, even hockey games. I have a hard enough time following the puck when I'm at a game, on the radio, man, it's impossible. When I'm in charge, it is eclectic city, you might find some sides by the Blasters mixed with Los Lobos or LCD Soundsystem or Sonny Rollins or Delbert McClinton. Toss in some Lyle Lovett, toss in some Steve Earle, some John Scofield and lots of Charlie Hunter. Aretha, Mavis Staples, Gatemouth Brown, Lowell Fulsom, whatever I do, it's got to be funky. But right now, as I tell my partner, "At this very moment, right here in 2005, I bet we're the only two Federal Agents in the US of A listening to Bob." Hell, I don't know for sure but the odds seem real good. And how you gonna check to prove me wrong? Besides, it gives us something to talk about while we wait for you know who.

"Prove it," he says.

Of course. "How?"

"We could call someone, say the dispatch for the FBI in Houston."

"What are they gonna do, an all points call — 'All agents, all agents, please report, anyone listening to Bob Marley?'"

Just so you know we could do that, call the Bureau. Hell, with our phony creds and our electronics we get all the radio traffic, we could call BATF (if you did call BATF you want to refer to them as ATF, only outsiders add the B even though it is officially part of their name), we could call ICE, we could call those drug guys from Don't Expect Anything (DEA). We can call Federal, State and local on both sides of the border. You'll see, later, we will be calling Border Patrol, maybe a few others. That's one of the reasons we're here.

"Statistical sampling," my partner says. "Send out a survey."

"Wouldn't the simple receipt of the survey cause someone to say they are listening to Bob Marley?"

"Like the Heisenberg Uncertainty Principle, the very act of observing changes."

"Yep, Heisenberg," which always makes me think of a hops laden German beer.

That's how, in the parlance of today's youth, we roll. We're all Heisenberg all the time, observation=action=change. In our present circumstances imagine this: a Government operation is off the books and, for whatever reason it has to be brought back onto the books, entered into the ledger so to speak. So, they send for our unit. They really don't have a glamorous name for us, nothing cool like CTU or UNCLE, just Unit 25. Yeah, sounds like a room on the second floor of the Bid-A-Wee Motel or a rental storage unit located off State Route 91. Informally, we came up with something else, we call ourselves the Footnote Guys, as in, "see, it wasn't off the books, it was in there all the time, guess you just didn't bother to read the footnotes." Sounds sexist, "Guys," but we've some women working here, hell, our boss is a woman, and they don't seem to mind being called a generic non-sex specific Guys, so you be cool with it.

What brings us to the border of Mexico and these here United States? On this bluff above the slow moving Rio Grande, where the smell of toxic and human waste merge and linger in the air? Is it just because of the good food and a chance for me to summon up a border music package — The Texas Tornadoes, Café Tacuba and the Nortec Collective — from my collection of jams? Just to view all the natural varieties of creosote bushes? What operation needs to be remanded? Simple, the Mexican Government has seen fit to provide Beto Taberas to the US Attorney's Office in Houston. And who is Beto Taberas? Beto is the devil. Really, the Devil. That's what ICE had him on the books as — Chamuco — "the Devil." You don't ordinarily refer to "controlled" informants under their real name, hence, the appropriate name for this particular piece of shoe sole dog turd — Chamuco. He could be a villain in the soap opera world of Mexican professional wrestling, wearing one of those decorated S&M masks, red cloth horns poking up, contending against the wily El Santo. Unfortunately, there's no fantasy morality play involved, he's our villain, originally caught by US Law Enforcement, de-hooked and released in native waters to attract a bigger fish, as if there are any bigger. Not snatched from some blue bucolic lake, nope, Chamuco was netted on the US side in Laredo, in the company of his money laundering cocaine consuming whore of a wife, his two over-weight children, Juan (10) and Ofelia (8), and about one and a half million dollars in ill-gotten gains. I say about because we both rounded down. Keep in mind this figure does not include what he still has in bank accounts both in the US and Panama, nor those bearer silver certificates squirreled away in a safe deposit box in Tucson.

Arresting a guy like Chamuco would headline any US Attorney's news conference, maybe even get the Attorney General to fly in and read something prepared especially for him, complete with phonetic spellings of all the big names and words, so he could read it right off the page. Chamuco was near the top of the Televisa Cartel. That alone makes him a genuine wall mounted trophy fish. Combine that with the fact that he also, over a fifteen-year period, had worked his way from a grunt at the Federal Highway Police to an office near the top FHP command.

How'd he rise so far? Simple, Camucho used his position with the FHP to protect his own Cartel's drug deals and to set up rivals, sometimes for busts, sometimes for death. This had the dual purpose of helping him rise simultaneously in both the ranks of the Cartel and the Police. Further, using his position in the FHP and the "Grupo Operativo" (Operations Group) of detectives and officers under his command, he hamstrung any investigations of the Televisa Cartel (though he allowed some minor seizures and arrests as cover). He and those under his command went balls to the walls on investigations involving the other cartels. One of those investigations resulted in the arrest and elimination of a rival, the regional National Police Chief Sandalio Gonzalez. Gonzalez had used his own position to protect the Ferre Cartel. Journalists touted Chamuco as an honest, humble policeman who could get things done. National politics beckoned. See, a real smart guy.

So why did the dumbass move across the border? Why leave his villas, his mistresses and his cohorts to come to the US? It was over a simple "business disagreement" with Cesar Santillan, the person directly above him in the Cartel. The disagreement was over a matter of "honor" and, just coincidently, a healthy sum of money. Acting under Chamuco's direction, the police seized a load of cocaine from a rival transporter, found in a hidden compartment welded beneath the trunk of the car along with a few hundred thousand in US dollars. Santillan believed, as a matter of honor, both the money and the dope were rightfully his.

Chamuco said, "Here's this fat fuck who does nothing but sit back and count the money I make for him telling me he wants both the product and the funds. Both."

Their discussion escalated.

"I have expenses, I told him. My guys need a taste. You are taking food from the mouth of my children."

Santillan was unwilling to listen to reason. The argument escalated.

"Perhaps this will convince you, I said, drawing my pistol. He tells me — "Chingate tu madre, carbon," that is what he says to me. Do you know this term?"

The agent did not.

"It is an insult. It means — Fuck your mother, you impotent incompetent shit. In all seriousness I tell you: I am able to perform sexually with many different women on the same day; my mother, God Bless her soul, was a saint and is now with the Lord; and I was very good at what I did. I earned a lot of money for this guy and this is how they treat me? It was unfair and demeaning so I shot him."

Camucho had left out some details. The body of Cesar Santillan was found, sans genitals, with burn marks up and down his arms and legs, and an opening the size of a boot toe where his left eye should be. The examiner noted that he was probably still alive when some of the early things took place, before slipping into an unconscious state. The eyeball was not found. Understand the Devil part now?

After his capture some dickhead from ICE had a plan. "We sent Camucho back," this pencil necked supervisor from ICE explained. "This way we could get the inside information, routes in and out, shipments, money, people."

I repeat, as if there was a bigger fish to be had.

Since 9/11, as our President likes to say, the world has changed. Here's one of the changes in law enforcement, drug dealers are bad but *9/10 bad*; the possibility of terrorists sneaking into the United States across the US — Mexico border is *9/12 bad* and *9/12 bad* trumps all else. Largely to make them relevant in the "War on Terror" DEA, FBI and other agencies have trumpeted the rise of narco-terrorists, moving through Latin America and across the border into the United States. These narco-terrorists are they same drug dealers that existed before Bin Laden et al, but now all that cocaine funds mansions with swimming pools and terrorism. Back in place, one of Camucho's roles was to be an early warning system for any terrorists with designs on entry. So the United States Government decided that a drug dealing, murderous piece of scum was a valuable asset in the on-going war on terrorism.

A reasonable man, Camucho agreed to return to Mexico, to re-man both his former legal and his illegal post. In exchange, his daughter was not sold into training for the border Donkey Show, his son was not sent to a pedophile ranch located within a two hour drive of Mexico City and his wife was not accidentally marked down as a trans-sexual, then sent to the men's prison.

Camucho dedicated himself to finding whoever did this horrible thing to Santillan, heading up both the Cartel's internal and the police's external investigation, controlling both sides. He was also ever vigilant, watching for that wave of terrorists who wanted to sneak over the border.

Remember the term they used — controlled informant? Camucho, absent the restraints of any fear of retribution was anything but controlled, he began operating as his own little kingdom, capturing and torturing rivals and those they employed. Some of the two years worth of torture may have been for information gathering, some likely for giggles, it resulted in numerous dead folks buried on the ranch grounds of what the papers have seen fit to call "Rancho De La Muerte." According to the Mexican papers, body parts, some with obvious teeth marks, were found in shallow graves scattered about the surrounding grounds. The ranch was immediately tied to Camucho and Camucho immediately told the investigating authorities that yes, he did these things but that he was acting under the authority of the US Government. This was, you can imagine, a surprise to the Mexican authorities, who had not been informed that Camucho's new role. It was also a surprise to the FBI and DEA, to some in the US Attorney's office, to just about everybody except one Assistant United States Attorney, two ICE agents and their supervisor. Hell, two of the bodies found on the Ranch of the Dead were highly placed informants of the DEA. A total body count of thirty was reconstructed, including nine women and six children. No known or suspected terrorists were among their numbers.

From our position, over the river, we could see activity across in Mexico. "Better get ready," my partner said. He left the passenger seat, opened the back door, reached in, removed the Beretta M501 Sniper Rifle from its cover.

As I mentioned before, the US Government is concerned about the possibility of terrorists sneaking across the border. Drugs, guns, people come across with impunity. It is a sieve. One of the ways to defeat a sieve is to plug a few holes.

You heard about the tunnels they've found under the border? They were in competition with the ones the US Government controls. Here's the new post 9/11 deal — we allow drugs and weapons and money to be sent through our tunnels so we can keep an eye on things. Usually drugs to the US, weapons to Mexico. And, money, well that runs both ways. You know the routes used by overland unlicensed workers? We've sought to eliminate all the routes not under our control. How? Sending out folks posing as banditos, stealing and beating and even raping, if that's what it takes to close down the route. For each route we close, another opens. You know, the border is a big place, hard to guard. Our latest idea is getting some outside help.

"Make the call," my partner said. Using the radio, I called the Border Patrol and reported a breach of the border, right where the Mexican National Police were to deliver us Camucho.

Over on the Mexican side, three Mexican military style Humvees entered the water, each had what appeared to be mounted machine guns. A fourth vehicle, an extended cab pick up with an open bed. Five uniformed soldiers, each carrying an AK-47 rode in the bed. The devil was not alone.

I looked them over through my binoculars. "Second one," I said to my partner. He sighted in and shot.

The rear tire of the second Humvee was no longer full of air.

People began jumping out of the Humvees. The water exploded with the activity of soldiers.

Two vehicles from the Border Patrol arrived on our side of the river, began to make their way down.

My partner fired a second shot, hitting one of the soldiers.

The Mexicans began firing at the Border Patrol vehicles. The agents stopped, sought cover behind their vehicle, begin to return fire.

Another group of trucks arrived on our side of the river. The US Patriot Police was a volunteer army patrolling the US Mexico border. Started by a bunch of rightwing gun enthusiasts, they like to capture undocumented workers, turn them over to the authorities so they can catch the same folks a few nights latter. Hey, we all have hobbies. The Patriot Patrol just happened to receive some large anonymous donations in support of their worthy cause, plugging some holes in the sieve. They had enough money to buy vehicles, weapons and to run some of their own patrols, and they always monitor the frequencies used by the Border Patrol. They too began to return fire on the Mexican soldiers.

My partner spots Camucho, he is looking up towards us, his hand shielding his eyes. His hand stays up, long moments after the top of his head rode a bullet train elsewhere.

My partner climbs back into the vehicle as The Blind Boys of Alabama are singing about the need for keeping the Devil way down in the hole. We begin driving away. Flurries of shots continue behind us.

"Sounds like someone finally made it to the machine guns."

"We need something here," I say to him, "something deep and profound." I try to come up with a phrase that meets those standards, only think of – 'Nice shooting Tex' and 'Heisenberg light, less killing, same bold flavor' – neither which I voice.

"Quien anda mal, termina mal."

"Come again?" I say.

"Bad things happen to people who deserve it."

We head toward a town, any town that has a bar. I imagine us sitting there, sipping our cold Negro Modelo beers, eating something spicy, discussing the next set of footnotes yet to be written.

BROKEN PROMISED LAND
By
CRAIG McDONALD

Davey James lit his third unfiltered Marlboro. He squinted at Luis DeCastro, sizing up the middle-aged Mexican who had just asked Davey to kill a woman.

This was clearly something dark and new for Luis, so it didn't take much imagination on Davey's part to envision how this dodgy proposition could go south in fast and ugly fashion.

Davey chewed his lip, took another hit from his cigarette, and then shotgunned his tequila. He waved at the barkeep and tapped the empty shot glass and the bigger empty beer glass next to it.

For his part, Luis DeCastro sipped his Bud Ice and fidgeted with a cardboard coaster emblazoned with an ad for "Poppers" — some kind of deep-fried/jalapeno/cream cheese appetizer.

Davey James had been touted to Luis DeCastro through channels: a ricochet recommendation via a friend who knew someone who knew somebody who knew this guy named Grapelli who did some business with this other guy named Davey James.

James blew smoke and smiled at the waitress as she handed him his tequila and a fresh pint of Tecate. When she was gone, he said, "Those were too fucking real, yeah?"

DeCastro swallowed and said, "Yeah."

Davey James snorted to himself and took a drink of his beer. "Yeah. So, Luis, you were saying, you've insured her?"

"Yeah. Some, here and there. I don't have a lot of money to invest in insurance, on account of..." Luis' voice trailed off.

"On account of she's in the workforce," Davey said, "and you're on the dole." He raised his thick dark eyebrows. "Right?"

Luis DeCastro stared at his hands. "Yes. That's it, pretty much."

"You insured just her?"

"No. It was cheaper just to go for a family deal."

"Better hope she doesn't have schemes on you then, my friend," Davey said.

Luis hesitated and then nodded. He didn't know what to say to that. He didn't like Davey James ... and he was scared of him. But he had come this far and couldn't imagine conducting another search like this one, so he had to swallow hard and see this negotiation through. *Get it done.*

"Okay," Davey said. "Some hypotheticals, just to be sure you can hang in on your end 'cause I so cherish my own fat ass. Right?"

Luis DeCastro licked his lips and nodded. He took another sip of Bud. "Okay. Go ahead."

Davey crossed his arms on the table and leaned in. "The cops come to you ... or maybe a private investigator, because the insurance companies sometimes employ them to snoop around a claim they think is ... suspicious. Yeah? You with me?"

"Sure."

"They say, 'Hey, Luis, mi amigo, your wife just got her sad-ass self killed. You started buying insurance for her, what … six months before her life took this last bloody turn? Sí? Why shouldn't we think maybe there is a connection?'" Davey James downed his fresh shot of tequila.

"How do you answer a puzzler like that, hombre?"

DeCastro looked around. "My son used to work here … right here at La Fiesta. And his friend, too. Both were shot to death about six months ago. We barely had the money to give my son a decent burial. Or his friend, Tommy, who didn't have a green card."

Davey grunted. "Old Tommy was an illegal?" He had visions of these two spic teens dying in a hail of bullets because of some drug deal gone south … some Narcotrafficante shit transplanted up north.

"Yes," Luis DeCastro said. "Tommy came across about six months before. Anyway, when it happened, we talked — my wife, Alexis, and me. It made us think. We both agreed to get our affairs in order. Both wrote our wills and had them notarized."

"That was very forward thinking of you, Luis. Very responsible. But mostly very visionary."

DeCastro smiled faintly. He hated this fat, greasy Italian.

"Well, okay. That's good news," Davey said. "That's very good news. I'm warming to your ability to hang in there. To tough it out." Davey James stroked his chin with a big hand. "'Alexis' — that don't sound too Mex' to me."

Luis DeCastro shook his head. "She's Dutch. Her father was first-generation American."

"Oh." Davey James squeezed the bridge of his nose with two big fingers. A white woman. *Hm.* Davey James shook loose another cigarette from his pack and dipped his hand into the right pocket of his sports jacket. He felt around — ignored the black plastic comb and the switchblade. He wrapped his big fingers around the old silver Zippo and fired up another. "When this is done, the cops will come to you to tell you that your wife has been found murdered. Can you look surprised when they do that? Can you look distraught?"

"I can. I'm sure I can," Luis said.

"I'm sure you can think about it and be ready to play the role," Davey said. "But can you do it and look convincing? Maybe fall down where you stand and look around, holding your hands up helplessly? Can you cry and shake and sob from the bottoms of your feet? Can you curl up and say nothing, just shaking and staring? I'm looking for a promise here: Can you truly play the part?"

"I can do these things."

"And then they're going to put you in a cruiser and take you to the morgue to identify her, probably. Unless there is someone else you can foist that dirty duty on."

"There's only us, now, since the boy…"

"Christ, that's too bad. Okay, Luis … you're going to have to look at your wife's body in the morgue and confirm it is her. You can do this thing?"

DeCastro swallowed hard. He took his first drink of Bud Ice that wasn't a half-assed sip. "How will you do it … do it … to her?"

"Good question," Davey said with a wink. "You want to know what you'll be looking at before you answer my question, right? That's fair." Davey sipped his beer. He dipped a hand into the bowl of tortilla chips between them and scooped up some salsa. "That's fair. You'll give me a photo of her. And descriptions of the family cars with their license plate numbers. Anything that could help me be sure I'm making the right … choice. Don't want to get the wrong broad here, am I right? I'll pick the moment and the place. It'll obviously be somewhere secluded. Maybe get her in a parking lot at night. I'll take her purse … maybe rip her blouse to make it look like some robbery and spontaneous sex thing. I could shoot her, but that might make it harder for cops to I.D. her with her purse gone… So I'll probably come up behind her. One hand over her mouth, and then I drag a knife across her neck. Slit her jugular and let her bleed out fast. Kinder that way, really. And it leaves less work for the undertaker so it may save you some bucks on that end." Davey winked. "See, I read you as a thrifty guy, Luis."

Davey James dipped his head low, watching Luis DeCastro. "You sure you can handle this?"

"I can." Luis DeCastro stared back into Davey James' searching eyes.

Davey tipped his head on side. "I believe you probably can. You got a picture of her?"

"I was told you might want one now," DeCastro said. He pulled out his raggedy, hand-tooled wallet and flipped through some acetate panels. He slid out a photo and handed it over. It was a picture of DeCastro, in sunglasses, standing with a boy in a mortar board — probably the dead son, photographed at the boy's high school graduation — and this blond woman with a sad smile and bruise on her cheek. She was thin and wore no sunglasses. Blue eyes … a generous but sad mouth. Good bone structure. Those haunted eyes.

"How did your boy die, exactly, Luis?"

"He and Tommy were robbing a house. They didn't clear the house properly. Some teenage boy got hold of a gun and 'went Rambo on them,' as the cops who told us put it."

Holy Christ, Davey thought, *so much for seeking the American dream*. Fucking family of beaner grifters. But he looked again at the photo: Luis DeCastro was staring at the camera with this death's head grin. His wife, Alexis, and their dead boy were beaming at one another, hugging. Luis stood apart.

Davey scowled. "I notice you don't use your boy's name much ... but I've heard 'Tommy' tossed around several times. You and your son weren't tight, I take it?"

"Not so close."

"But you liked Tommy?"

"I did. He was still ... he reminded me of home."

"By that you mean he reminded you of yourself."

"He didn't try to be American," Luis said.

"Didn't assimilate, huh?" Davey shook his head. "Christ. Do I look like a 'Davey James'? Last name, before my folks changed it when they came over, was 'Canaletto.' My middle name is James. I'm really 'Giulio.' You're fucking supposed to blend in, Luis." He gestured with a big hand at the restaurant's faux-Mexican trappings and at his own bottle of Tecate. "When in Rome, amigo..."

The old Latino shrugged. "Tommy was better company."

"Than your own son?" Davey's own deadbeat old man had always favored Davey's friend, Angelo.

Luis was listening to the jukebox now: Harry Dean Stanton was singing "Canción Mixteca":

"Y al verme tan solo y triste cual hoja al viento/ quisiera llorar, quisiera mori/ de sentimiento.

Davey said, "You like that song?"

Luis shrugged. "It's about Mexico: 'How far I am from the land where I was born/ Immense sadness fills my thoughts/ I see myself so alone and so sad/ Like a leaf in the wind.'"

The big man grunted: "You miss Mexico so goddamned much, why don't you go back?"

The Mexican's fingernail scratched with little result at the label on his bottle of Bud Ice. "Because there's even less for me there than there is for me here."

Davey thought maybe that remained to be seen. But he said, "Who planned the heist that went bad? Tommy? Your boy? You and Tommy? Or maybe just you?"

"I helped them plan some," Luis DeCastro said.

Davey winked. "Still got a hand in that game?"

Luis shrugged — probably thought he was bonding with Davey by sharing criminal histories. "A bit here and there. I offer some tips to some young guys coming up ... they pay me a bit on the other end toward future advice." Davey smiled and shook his head: *Jesus H., I'm seated across from the Fagin of the barrios.*

He looked again at Alexis DeCastro. Hell, one hundred and fifty pounds ago, he might have had a shot at a woman like that. Hell, if she was living with a sorry piece of work like Luis, Davey thought he might still have a shot. "What's with this bruise on her cheek?" Davey tried to sound nonchalant: "She spout off and you have to cuff the bitch?"

DeCastro smiled faintly.

Aha. Davey decided to press a little ... figured he deserved it if he was going to take money to kill this poor beaten-on woman. "Why do you want to murder your wife, Luis? Strictly a money thing?"

"Mostly."

"Don't you love her — even a little — anymore?"

"What do you care?" "Just curious. Figure I'm entitled. Do you love her any?"

"No. Not at all. Never did, really. If she would have had the abortion..."

"She brings home a paycheck, yeah? She cook for you, too?"

"She makes dinner and breakfast every day ... not much variety, either."

"Leaves you to fend for yourself for lunch, yeah? That's shitty." Davey smiled. "Me, I eat on the run. Fast food and shit. Why I look like I do. Don't remember my last home-cooked meal. What's her best dinner? What's her specialty?"

"What is this?"

Davey leaned in again: "Hey, Pancho, I'm gonna punch your old lady's ticket for you, and on the cheap at that, 'cause I'm being keistered by some Warren loanshark and need the jack, you know? So I figure I get a few questions, jerk-off."

"You've had them," DeCastro said. He tried to come across as a hard case: "Two thousand now ... two thousand more when I get the insurance check. Take it or leave it, David."

"Oh, I'll take it," Davey said. He pulled out a small notepad and ballpoint pen and tossed them at Luis DeCastro: "Makes and models of your cars and license plates there, amigo ... assuming you can write in English."

Luis scribbled away. He handed the notebook back to Davey James: better than Davey's own penmanship.

DeCastro, an edge in his voice: "How many women have you killed, David?"

The big man shrugged. Why lie? Davey said, "Your wife would be my first."

"Why? Why none before this?"

"Guess I never needed the money bad enough. Think you'll miss her later, Luis? Have regrets?"

Luis DeCastro sneered. "I dunno: You sure you can do this thing for me? Sure you won't disappoint me?"

Davey moved fast, gripping the back of Luis DeCastro's neck in his big hand. "One more word, and I'll make you a part of this table top. Yeah?" His grip tightened.

Luis winced and grimaced. He said in a hoarse voice, "Yes…"

"Don't ever put a question like that to me again, Luis. That could be something worse than a deal-breaker." Then Davey smiled and released Luis DeCastro's neck. Davey picked up the notepad and shoved it back into the interior breast pocket of his sports jacket. He suddenly swatted the pocket and dipped his hand back in. "Christ," he said. "Damned phone." He reached in and plucked out his cell. He held it up and it was flashing and vibrating. "Gotta get this. Be right back." Opening the cell phone, he rose and walked out into the parking lot.

When he was outside, Davey flipped closed the cell phone and dropped it back in his pocket. He looked again at the photo, studying Alexis DeCastro's face … her eyes and smile. He tried to imagine shutting out her fragile light.

Davey pulled out the notebook he had handed Luis — the notebook he had thrust into the same jacket pocket as his phone in order to press the button that would make it vibrate. He checked the license plate number written there and found Luis DeCastro's wheels — a dented Ford Aerostar mini-van. Davey's hand dipped into his right hand pocket and wrapped around the switchblade. He settled on the rear driver's side tire.

When he got back inside, it was obvious to Davey that Luis DeCastro had found some reservoir of courage … maybe

Luis found it in his bottle of Bud Ice. Luis said, "You gonna do this thing, or not? I need an answer, now, David."

If not Davey, it would be another. Davey sat back down and drained the dregs of his Tecate. "Oh, I'm gonna take good care of her. Promise."

Davey held out his hand, and Luis passed him a wrinkled bank envelope — the first two thousand. Davey opened the end of the envelope, rifled through twenty and hundred dollar bills with a thumbnail, then re-sealed the envelope and slipped it into the pocket of his sports jacket.

Luis raised his eyebrow. "You're not going to count it?"

"No. 'Cause I know where to find you, Luis." He slapped Luis' flabby arm. "C'mon, amigo, I'll walk you out," Davey said.

They settled up and threaded their way through the bar back to the parking lot. It was dusk now and bugs flew in the cones cast by the too-few parking lot lights.

Davey looked around: Nobody was coming or going.

The two men had arrived separately. Luis DeCastro had no way of knowing what kind of car Davey James drove or where it was parked, so it didn't bother Luis that Davey stayed right at his heels.

As they neared the Aerostar, now listing to one side, Luis DeCastro cursed. He moved around to the back of his van and squatted, inspecting the wheel. "Fucking tire is flat."

Davey James clucked his tongue and moved around behind Luis to inspect the wheel. "That's flat alright, Luis. Tortilla flat, even. Spare is in the back?" His hand dipped into his right pocket. "C'mon, back here," Davey said to Luis DeCastro. "I'll help you fix her up."

PART II

BORDERLAND (FILM) NOIR

Won't someone roll the credits
on 20 years of love gone dark and raw?
It's not a Technicolor love film
(it's a brutal document — it's film noir)
It's all played out on a borderline
where the actors are tragically miscast.
— Tom Russell
"Touch of Evil"

Conventional wisdom among film critics has it Orson Welles' *Touch of Evil* marks the last true, first-wave entry in the film noir genre. Arguably, along with *The Treasure of the Sierra Madre* — based on the novel of the same name by the über mysterious B. Traven (more on him, later) — *Evil* also stands as one of the first Borderland (film) Noirs. In the following essay, crime novelist Dave Zeltserman considers one of Welles' greatest films. (*Caution*: Spoilers abound.) —CM

"All border towns bring out the worst in a country."
—Miguel "Mike" Vargas

TOUCH OF EVIL
By
DAVE ZELTSERMAN

In 1957 Universal Studios sent Orson Welles a script based loosely on Whit Masterson's* *Badge of Evil,* asking if he'd play the part of the crooked detective. According to Welles, the script was a very bad one, with not much in it other than a detective with a good record who plants evidence because he knows somebody is guilty — and the fellow turns out to be really guilty. But Welles needed the money and agreed to do it.

Universal then called up Charlton Heston who at the time was coming off the success of *The Ten Commandments,* and told him "Here's a script — we'd like you to read it. We have Welles."

Heston misunderstood and responded, "Well, any picture that Welles directs, I'll make." Universal, instead of correcting this misunderstanding, asked Welles if he'd direct. Welles agreed under the condition that he could rewrite the script. Universal let him do it, but would only pay him his original salary as an actor (one hundred and twenty five thousand dollars) and not as a director or writer. And so was born *Touch of Evil.*

The opening sequence is the most famous in the movie: a three minute and twenty second uninterrupted crane tracking shot that follows a shadowy figure placing a bomb in a car and then an unsuspecting couple — a wealthy American businessman and his stripper girlfriend — entering the car and driving towards the US-Mexican border four blocks away, all the while (due to traffic, donkeys in the street, etc.) keeping pace with Miguel and Susan Vargas (Charlton Heston and Janet Leigh), newlyweds who are heading to the US side of the border in search of a chocolate soda. It isn't until the car enters the US side of the border that the car separates from Vargas and his wife and explodes into a deadly fireball.

While the bomb was planted on Mexican soil (a fictitious town called Los Robles which was patterned after Tijuana), the explosion occurred in the US, and is to be investigated by US officials. Vargas, a top Mexico City narcotics investigator, hangs around to offer his assistance as the police wait for Hank Quinlan to arrive. Orson Welles was 42 when *Touch of Evil* was filmed, but with the makeup to make his face appear swollen and bloated, the padding under his ever-present overcoat, the thick cane he relies on and the camera angles to make his heft appear far heavier, Welles' Quinlan is massive. A bloated monstrosity of a man who looks like he's in his late sixties (another hint of his age is his wife had been murdered — strangled to death — thirty years earlier, the killer being the only criminal to escape Quinlan's justice).

When Quinlan arrives at the scene he makes quick intuitive guesses as to what happened and what needs to be investigated. Quinlan is a man of intuition and expediency while Vargas is more of a technocrat, a by-the-numbers straight-laced cop. Quinlan leads an expedition to the Mexican side of the border, a tawdry area lined with bars, strip clubs and brothels. Quinlan and his fellow cops descend on the strip club where the dead stripper had worked, eager to catch glimpses of naked flesh inside. In an alley outside the club, Vargas is attacked by one of the Grandi gang members (a parallel story is one of the Grandi gang trying to intimidate Vargas to drop a case against their patriarch), who throws acid at Vargas's face. In Welles' original script, the acid misses Vargas and hits a cat asleep in the trash. This was changed in the film and the acid instead explodes in a smoky hiss against the poster of the dead stripper.

As Quinlan leaves the back entrance of the Rancho Grande strip club, he is stopped by pianola music coming from a local brothel run by Marlene Dietrich (Universal Studios was later surprised and delighted to learn that Dietrich was in the film. They ended up paying her so they could give her billing, but she had been willing to be in it unbilled as a favor to Welles). Dietrich's brothel is a place of another era, complete with its pianola, mounted bull's head on the wall, and other aging artifacts. It's a place that Hemingway might've been comfortable in. Or Welles. As it is, it has been years since Quinlan had visited Tanya's (Marlene Dietrich) brothel, and at first she doesn't recognize him. When Quinlan wistfully identifies himself, Tanya prophetically warns him that he should lay off the candy bars. Even under all the padding and with camera angles to accentuate Quinlan's bulk, Welles was still a large man when he made *Touch of Evil* (although he was going to get much larger) and he should've heeded that warning.

While Vargas is aiding in the investigation, Quinlan's partner Pete Menzies (played touchingly by Joseph Calleia) drives Susan Vargas to the Mirador Motel for protection against the Grandi gang (although, as it turns out the motel is owned by the Grandis) and to wait for her husband. The motel is both isolated and seedy, and the night clerk is played brilliantly by Dennis Weaver. Weaver's night clerk is a mass of spasms, twitches and leers. Someone who can barely make eye contact and jumps when Susan Vargas asks if he can make the bed, barking out the single question "Bed?" in return as if it were something fearsome and unholy. One can only wonder if watching *Touch of Evil* gave Hitchcock the idea of putting Janet Leigh in yet another bad motel setting.

Quinlan's intuition leads him to suspect the dead man's daughter's boyfriend, a Mexican shoe clerk named Manolo Sanchez. Quinlan brings his fellow cops and prosecutors to Sanchez's claustrophobic shoebox-sized apartment, and then performs his sleight-of-hand—hiding sticks of dynamite in a box so his unsuspecting partner will find them. As Quinlan waits for the dynamite to be discovered, he's an entertainer, amused by his own trickery. The problem though is the magic trick has been revealed — Vargas had used the bathroom and knocked over the box where Quinlan later had planted the dynamite. He knows the box had been empty. He knows what Quinlan has done. The great magician has been exposed as a fake — and Quinlan's reputation is in jeopardy of being destroyed. Quinlan is a corrupt cop but his motivation is because he knows he is greater than those mere mortals around him. He is doing nothing more than speeding up the convictions of the guilty. He doesn't financially profit from his corruption. In fact, later he demands from his partner, what has he got in life, a few acres and a turkey ranch? Critic Andre Bazin describes Quinlan as such:

"Quinlan is physically monstrous, but is he morally monstrous? The answer is yes and no. Yes, because he is guilty of committing a crime to defend himself; no because from a higher moral standpoint, he is, at least in certain respects, above the honest, just, intelligent Vargas, who will always lack the sense of life which I call Shakespearean. These exceptional beings should not be judged by ordinary laws. They are both weaker and stronger than others. Weaker... [but] also so much stronger because directly in touch with the true nature of things, or perhaps one should say, with God."

Facing exposure and ruin, Quinlan enters an agreement with "Uncle" Joe Grandi, the new head of the Grandi organization. Joe Grandi, as played by Akim Tamiroff, is a wannabe Edward G. Robinson-type gangster, but is only comical and pathetic. An earlier scene has him running around with his toupee half off. Uncle Joe's plan is to frame Susan Vargas on trumped drug charges — back at the Mirador Motel his gang had invaded Susan's room with a butched-up Mercedes McCambridge begging to be able to watch as gang members grab Susan's legs as she's dolled out in a negligee. Quinlan is now drinking for the first time in years, waiting until the last moment to go along with Uncle Joe's plans (in fact calling up headquarters at the last possible moment to see if Sanchez has confessed yet — he may have framed him, but he intuitively knows the man is guilty). When Quinlan finally enters the cheap downtown hotel room where Grandi had Susan brought, she is in bed, unconscious, with reefers and heroin needles scattered about the room (as a concession to the times and the censors, she had been drugged with sodium pentothal — with nothing else done to her. Come on! Sodium pentothal? In real life, she would've been shot up with heroin, and each of the gang members — including Mercedes McCambridge would've had a turn with her!). Quinlan has other plans — namely to strangle Uncle Joe and leave his body with Susan. Quinlan's actual murder of Uncle Joe is a gruesome, violent scene, intentionally sexually charged. As Welles said in conversations with Peter Bogdanovich** "It was perverse and morbid... one of those go-as-far-as-you-can-go — in that kind of dirty department... when [Tamiroff] looked at the gun, it was every cock in the world. It was awful, the way he looked at it — made the whole scene possible." Make no mistake about it, this is an ugly scene. Tamiroff is a much smaller man than Welles, and is just about consumed by Welles. Tamiroff's character is dragged around the room, his shirt torn at the chest, his toupee knocked off. Eventually Quinlan strangles him with one of Susan's stockings, leaving Uncle Joe's face hanging over the bed, eyes bulging out by a nice effect of using painted contact lenses. Welles wanted the shot of the bulging eyes short enough so it would be almost subliminal—something people wouldn't be quite sure they saw—but the studio added extra frames to that shot. More on that later. When Quinlan leaves the room a close up of a sign on the door reads:

Stop, Forget Anything, Leave Key at Desk.

After Quinlan leaves, Susan Vargas wakes up from her sodium pentothal-induced stupor to see Uncle Joe's dead bulging eyes staring at her and she runs screaming to the balcony. Later, after she's been arrested, Pete Menzies confronts Vargas. Quinlan had forgotten something in the hotel room. His cane. And Menzies had found it. He can no longer ignore the fact that he's been an unwitting dupe in framing scores of criminals (probably all guilty). He agrees to help Vargas uncover the truth about Quinlan by wearing a recording device. After the murder, Quinlan had holed up at Tanya's brothel. Drunk, he asks her to read his fortune. She tells him he has no future, it's been used up. Menzies later lures Quinlan out of the brothel so he can coax a confession out of him. Quinlan leads Menzies along a desolated area along the canal and oil derricks, while Vargas has to climb mountains of trash and wade through filth to try to record Quinlan's guilt. Eventually Quinlan incriminates himself, but with Vargas and his recording equipment under a bridge, an echo can be heard of Quinlan's voice, leading Quinlan to realize the level of betrayal. Quinlan shoots Menzies and then tries to kill Vargas before being shot by his dying partner. After Quinlan is shot he tells his partner that's the second bullet he's taken for him. For years that line puzzled viewers. The reason for that was in Welles original version, Menzies had earlier told Susan Vargas how Quinlan had taken a bullet for him — saved his life, but left Quinlan with his limp and needing his cane. The studio-edited version had cut the scene, and it wasn't until the 1998 version was released that the scene was re-added and Quinlan's last mocking line made sense. After being shot, Quinlan falls backward into the canal and the filth where he dies. Tanya arrives at the scene with the DA (who announces that Sanchez confessed to the crime after all) and provides as a eulogy to Quinlan: "He was some kind of a man. What does it matter what you say about people?"

Welles on Quinlan's betrayal***:

"Quinlan is [Menzies's] God. And as Menzies adores him, the real theme of the script is betrayal; the terrible necessity for Menzies to betray his friend. And that's where there is ambiguity, because I don't know whether he should have betrayed him or not. No, I really don't know. I force Menzies to betray him, but the decision does not come from him, and frankly, in his place, I would not have done it!"

While Welles was making *Touch of Evil* he was under the impression that he was going to be making more movies for Universal, that *Touch of Evil* was going to be his entry back into Hollywood. When the studio saw his final cut version, he was fired as director and barred from the lot. *Touch of Evil* is a wonderfully dark movie, but for 1958, it was probably too dark and too strange for Hollywood, and it hit on difficult themes: police corruption, racism and drugs. The studio must have felt as betrayed by Welles as he did by the studio. While

Welles would make other films, notably *Chimes at Midnight*, *The Trial* and *F is for Fake* (along with a slew of half-finished films), this would be Welles last Hollywood film. And as a final act of betrayal, the studio re-edited *Touch of Evil*.

Welles would later write a fifty six-page memo requesting changes back to his original film, which the studio ignored (the 1998 version attempted to restore the movie according to Welles memo). Funny how art mirrors life.

* Whit Masterson was a pseudonym for Wade Miller—aka Robert Wade and William Miller.

** From This Is Orson Welles by Orson Welles and Peter Bogdanovich

*** From Orson Welles Interviews edited by Mark W. Estrin

PART III

THE CENTAUR OF THE NORTH

Don't let it end like this.
Tell them I said something.
—Pancho Villa's purported last words

The "friction between Old Me-hi-co and El Norte" starts here: You'd be hard-pressed to find a badder bastard than the bandit-general who attacked the U.S. and evaded the U.S. Army — only to be rubbed out in a political hit on the streets of Parral. —JC

PANCHO VILLA—FOURTH HORSMAN OF THE MEXICAN APOCALYPSE

By
JIM CORNELIUS

(Outside Ciudad Chihuhua, November 13, 1913)

Ciudad Chihuhua was a proving to be tough nut to crack.

General Francisco "Pancho" Villa had taken other cities in the vast Northern Mexico state in his effort to overthrow the military dictatorship of Victoriano Huerta. But the state capital was fiercely resisting his assaults. His former comrade Pascual Orozco and his private force of Colorados, known for their blood-red flag, were putting up a stiffer fight than the Federal troops — mostly conscripts — usually did, and Pancho was losing men. This wasn't working.

But Villa had a plan.

That night, he led 2,000 cavalrymen on a thundering sweep around Ciudad Chihuahua toward a copper foundry on the outskirts of the city. There, his force intercepted a south-bound coal train and captured a telegraph operator. Pancho put a pistol to his head and gave him a message to relay back to Juarez on the U.S. Mexican border: The train was derailed and the countryside was swarming with Villista rebels.

Just as Villa hoped, orders came down to repair the engine and roll back up the line to Juarez, checking in at each station along the way.

The Villistas dumped the coal from the train, loaded their horses and climbed aboard. At each station, the telegraph operator, sweating and staring down the big bore of Pancho Villa's .45 Bisley Colt, checked in and received orders to proceed. In the early hours of November 15, the train — like Bob Dylan's "Wanted Man" — rolled the wrong way into Juarez.

Juarez was rolling at full roar, its casinos and cantinas packed with locals and American touristas indulging their appetites for every kind of vice, from cards and dice to booze and whores. The Trojan train steamed into the station and disgorged a couple of thousand hard-bitten Villista revolutionaries. One contingent stormed off to take over the casinos, where they expropriated a massive donation in silver for the cause. Another troop peeled off to seize control of the police station, the federal garrison and the international bridges.

There was hardly any resistance. Orozco partisans fled the city in disarray, and when a few came back to stage a counterattack, the Villistas drove them off. The police headquarters and the garrison held out for a little while, but ultimately gave up the prize. With minimal casualties, Pancho Villa had seized one of Chihuahua's biggest cities, scored a massive financial windfall and had established a conduit for smuggled arms and legitimately purchased military and medical supplies.

Villa was now the most powerful warlord in northern Mexico — and an international superstar.

Francisco Villa was a bandit. There might be some arguments whether he was a villain or a hero, a madman or a genius, but everyone agreed he was a bandit...
—William Webster Johnson, "Heroic Mexico"

Pancho Villa was the kind of man around whom legends gather. During his lifetime, hundreds of *corridos*—Mexican narrative ballads—sang his story, from his days as a bandit riding the sierra to his pinnacle of power as the commander of the mightiest fighting force in the Western Hemisphere. To this day, he remains a figure of legend and controversy. Was he a hero or a villain, a freedom fighter or a terrorist? The not-so-simple answer is: Yes.

Just as there is no argument that Villa was a bandit, it is also beyond doubt is that he was a highly capable frontier partisan warrior. He honed the fundamental skills during his bandit days, becoming a deadly marksman and a breathtaking horseman. Not for nothing did they call him the Centaur of the North.

His biographer Friedrich Katz, says: "Villa had the reputation of being one of Mexico's greatest gunfighters. 'For Villa, the gun was more important than eating or sleeping,' a subordinate wrote about him. 'It was a part of his person indispensable to him wherever he was, even at social occasions, and one can say that it was only very rarely that he did not have a gun ready to be drawn or placed in his gunbelt.'

"(Another contemporary observed): 'He is a remarkable horseman, sits on his horse with cowboy ease and grace, rides straight and stiff-legged Mexican style, and would only use a Mexican saddle. He loves his horse, is very considerate of his comfort, probably due to the fact that they have aided him in escaping from tight places so many times. He has often ridden over a hundred miles within 24 hours over the roughest mountain trails…'"

So Villa liked his guns and he loved his horses. And he loved women. Many women. But the bandit was no cad. He believed in marriage, and he took his women to the altar — one after another.

The Mexican Revolution was a complex and deadly brew of power-lust, idealism, betrayal and conspiracy. No game of thrones was ever more violent and deadly. Every one of its major leaders died violently. All factions executed prisoners by firing squad and civilians often suffered abuse or atrocity at the hands of federals or rebels — or each in turn.

However, Villa's Division del Norte was exceptionally disciplined. While he did confiscate land and money from those he deemed enemies of the Revolution, Villa forbade drunkenness and looting and was especially careful to protect American property. He was, after all, receiving funds and arms from the north and he did not want to alienate the Americans. The general outfitted his military trains with medical cars, rolling hospitals with the latest equipment and the best medical professionals. Villa was a genuine friend of the poor and he was especially committed to building schools and seeing to it that children in his area of operations received an education.

Though he would degenerate morally under the pressures of defeat and the increasing savagery of what would soon become a civil war, Villa during the 1910-1914 Revolution lived down his fearsome reputation as a bandit.

At the Revolution's start in 1910, Francisco Villa was weaving along the indistinct line between solid citizen and outlaw, operating a butcher shop in Chihuahua — and supplying it with rustled beef.

Legend has it that young Doroteo Arango hit the outlaw trail after he killed a hacendado's son who had raped his sister. He then took the nom de guerre of a famous bandit named Francisco Villa. The legend may be true. There were plenty of reasons for a young man from a poor family to turn bandit during the 30-year rule of Porfirio Diaz.

Diaz was a modernizer and he dragged Mexico into the 19th and 20th centuries—but he wasn't gentle about it. He allowed the hacendados, owners of vast estates that encompassed square miles of territory, to expropriate more and more land, forcing peasants deeper into something very close to slavery. Diaz cracked down hard on labor unrest in Mexico's burgeoning industrial sector, and the mines were nothing short of a circle of hell.

The rural poor had it hard, and the only way to live a free life was to live it outside the law. That life was usually brutal and short. An hombre was liable to catch a bullet from the bandits-turned-police of the rural guard — Diaz's feared Rurales. Villa did better than most. Sometimes he was a bandit, sometimes he guarded ore shipments for American companies against bandits.

By 1910, at age 32, he was semi-respectable, though he still maintained contacts on the wrong side of the law. Something like a Mafioso, he was a man to be reckoned with — a man you wanted on your side if political agitation came to shooting.

He was swept up by the revolutionary fervor of Abraham Gonzalez and Francisco Madero, classic liberal reformers driven to arms by the intransigent dictatorship of Porfirio Diaz. Villa would distinguish himself as a gifted leader of irregular cavalry and a charismatic commander of a hodge-podge of revolutionary forces.

Along with former muleskinner Pascual Orozco, Villa won the key victory of the 1910 Revolution in the Battle of Juarez. Americans in El Paso climbed up on boxcars and sipped beer on hotel rooftops as they watched the fighting across the Rio Grande.

Francisco Madero became president with the promise of reforms that would raise the stature of the poor in Mexican society. Then as now, hope and change were easier to promise than to deliver. Madero was soon assailed by a rebellion by Emiliano Zapata in the south, frustrated by the slow pace of land reform. In the north, Orozco rebelled, too, financed by the old regime hacendados who felt their power slipping away.

Villa stood by Madero and soon he and Orozco were at each other's throats. Again, Villa proved himself a wily commander and vicious fighter, scoring lighting victories in a campaign that ranged across the northern tier of Mexico.

Madero had kept Diaz's federal army intact and a Porfirista general named Victoriano Huerta led the effort to suppress the Orozco rebellion. Huerta was a sonofabitch if there ever was one, devious and mean, with a bottomless capacity for treachery and Napoleon brandy. He held Madero in contempt and he hated irregulars in general and Francisco Villa in particular.

Pancho was fond of good horseflesh and commandeered a horse during one of his operations. Huerta accused him of brigandage, had him dragged out of a hotel room shaking and half-delirious with fever and had him stood up against a wall. Villa, as he was prone to do in moments of stress, broke into tears of rage and frustration, a humiliation he would not forget. The intervention of one of Madero's brothers saved him from the firing squad and instead he was carted off to prison in Mexico City. There he had a bed installed in his cell, where he availed himself of Mexico's liberal (and humane) attitude toward conjugal visits, learned to write his name and read (or had read to him) "Don Quixote" and the swashbuckling tales of Alexandre Dumas.

A group of plotters tried to enlist him in a coup against Madero, but Villa truly was loyal to the hapless little presidente and he not only declined, but escaped from prison and made his way to El Paso, where he sent word to his mentor Abraham Gonzalez, now Governor of Chihuahua, that he stood ready to defend Madero and his revolution.

Huerta had Madero and his vice president whacked and seized power. His minions threw Gonzalez under the wheels of a moving train.

Pancho Villa was seriously pissed. In March of 1913, Villa, with a handful of followers, crossed the Rio Grande and announced that he was coming after Huerta. Game on...

It was one of the most remarkable feats in the annals of frontier partisan warfare — hell, in all of military history.

In March 1913, Pancho Villa crossed the border from the U.S. into Mexico leading eight men. He sent a telegram to the Huertista governor of Chihuahua, General Antonio Rabago:

"Knowing that the government you represent was preparing to extradite me, I decided to come here and save you the bother. Here I am in Mexico, resolved to make war upon the tyranny which you defend. Francisco Villa."

He proceeded to do just that. Gathering followers, first by the handful, then by the hundreds, he raided haciendas and hijacked trains, once capturing a shipment of 122 bars of silver. He traded rustled cattle and stolen silver for arms in the United States.

In a year's time, he had built commanded the mightiest army in the western hemisphere, the storied Division del Norte, storming into the Mexican heartland, moving from triumph to triumph to overthrow the usurper, Victoriano Huerta.

The strategically critical objective of the revolutionary war in Chihuahua was control of the railway that ran from the U.S. border at El Paso down into the interior and eventually to Mexico City. Villa employed night attacks and cunning misdirection to take the garrisons of cities on that route.

Abandoning the faltering siege of Ciudad Chihuahua for his sneak attack on Juarez was perhaps his greatest military feat.

With that special operations coup, the bandit general controlled the vital border point of entry for supplies of arms and other materiel of war, and gained the notice of the United States and the international community. The brilliance of the operation and the new strength of his position also attracted talent to his force.

Villa's Division del Norte was made up of cowboys and miners, idealistic intellectuals and disgruntled federal officers, like the brilliant Felipe Angeles, who commanded Villa's growing artillery contingent. Angeles was a noble soul, whose social-democratic outlook would have fit right in with the European intelligentsia of the day. It also attracted natural-born killers, like Villa's old compadre of the Sierra Madre from his bandit days, Tomas Urbina, and the man who would become Villa's bodyguard, head of railroad operations and executioner, Rodolfo Fierro.

Immediately after the capture of Juarez, Villa marched south to meet a substantial federal force at Tierra Blanca. In a skillfully conducted battle, he routed the Federales. Like a Western movie hero, Fierro rode down an escaping federal train, jumped aboard, shot the engineer and slammed on the brakes. The triumphant Villistas swarmed aboard and slaughtered the hapless troops.

That victory opened the way to the south. Ciudad Chihuahua finally fell, and Villa was on the march to Mexico City.

And he would have more trouble with infighting on his own side than he would with the battered federal army.

The general had placed himself under the civilian control of Venustiano Carranza, the self-proclaimed First Chief of the Constitutionalist faction that was seeking Huerta's overthrow. It was an unhappy relationship. Carranza, vain, aristocratic and inscrutable, disdained the rough bandit chieftain from the sierra, even as that bandit won the big battles that would throw Huerta out of power. He couldn't bear to watch the ascendancy of a crude peasant with an underslung jaw, and as Villa's star rose, Carranza began undermining his authority and impeding his military momentum.

He diverted coal trains away from Villa to stop his march on the federal bastion at the mountain silver mining town of Zacatecas. He encouraged Villa's officers to mutiny. Villa, in a fit of emotionalism, threatened to resign, threatened to shoot himself and also offered a mutual suicide pact with Carranza for the good of the Revolution (The Bearded One declined).

The First Chief's ploy backfired, with Villa's subordinates reaffirming their loyalty and the Division del Norte marching on Zacatecas for the most titanic battle of the first phase of the Revolution.

General Angeles deployed Villa's artillery to bombard two hilltop fortresses, La Bufa and El Grillo, that guarded Zacatecas, and with that artillery support Villa's infantry stormed the strongpoints and took them in a welter of blood. The slaughter had just begun. The Villistas rained fire down on the red tile roofs of Zacatecas. The Federals began to flee, blowing up their arsenal, leveling a full city block and killing some 300 civilians.

The garrison's retreat took them through a ravine south of the city. Villistas circled around the city and lined the narrowing ravine, opening up a withering crossfire with Mausers and machine guns. The trapped Federales died in heaps, unable to fight, unable to flee. Surrender was the only option. Common soldiers were offered the choice of a bullet or service under Villa; officers were taken to the Zacatecas cemetery where firing squads overheated their Mauser barrels with wholesale executions.

The Mexican Federal Army lost six thousand to seven thousand soldiers while the conquering Villistas suffered about seven hundred dead and took one thousand five hundred wounded. Toma de Zacatecas was the greatest triumph of the Revolution.

The battle broke Huerta, who fled into exile. For a moment, the people's Revolution was triumphant. Then it all went to hell. Following the tragic pattern of so many 20th Century revolutions, the triumph over tyranny almost immediately disintegrated in a welter of personal ambition, petty feuds and jockeying for power. After a complicated round of conventions and political infighting, Carranza abandoned the capital. Villa marched into Mexico City in December, 1914, to meet the southern guerrilla army of Emiliano Zapata, another charismatic and picturesque peasant general who had fought stubbornly to overthrow federal control of his native province of Morelos.

Civil war loomed, and it would be far more savage than the revolutionary conflict. In early 1915, Carranza's favored general, Alvaro Obregon, squared off against the triumphant Villa, who looked invincible.

But Villa had a unique capacity for snatching defeat from the jaws of victory. The same audacity that had allowed him to spit defiance with only eight men at his back made him over-confident at the head of 20,000. Obregon, a canny customer, was paying close attention to the military developments of the First World War raging across Europe, and he had German advisors who helped refine the lessons of the Western Front and apply them to the Mexican Civil War.

In April 1915, Obregon provoked the mercurial Villa into two battles at Celaya in the Laguna country in the center of Mexico. The first engagement was inconclusive. The second was a shattering defeat for Villa. In the biggest battle in the western hemisphere since Gettysburg, Obregon smashed the Division del Norte.

Some have argued that Celaya marked the failure of machismo in the face of interlocking fields of fire and to some extent, that's true. Villa thrived on the offensive, he believed himself born to attack and attack he did, into machine guns, flooded cotton fields and trenches. Like Lee at Gettysburg, he believed his troops capable of doing the impossible. They proved not to be invincible after all. They were flesh and blood, to be rent and broken by a storm of steel.

But it must be noted Villa's failure at Celaya was little different from that of the British at the Somme or the Germans at Verdun. Tactics for attack had not evolved a solution for the sheer potency of prepared defensive positions (trenches and barbed wire) and firepower. Attacks could break into a defended line, but could not hold in the face of counterattack.

Villa limped away, only to be goaded into another battle at the city of Leon. The battle there lasted 40 days and closely replicated the hellishness Western Front. Again, Villa was beaten.

It was all downhill from there. The general rallied the remnants of his command and marched across the Sierra Madre into Sonora, hoping to change his fortunes by taking the Carrancista garrison at the border town of Agua Prieta. But by this time, the U.S. had decided to recognize Carranza's government and they allowed the transport of Carrancista reinforcements across U.S. territory. When Villa launched a night attack on the city's defenses, searchlights powered by electricity run across the border lit up the desert and spotlighted Villa's men, who were again mowed down in droves.

After a last fight deeper in Sonora, Villa disbanded the tattered remains of the Division del Norte, and with a handful of loyal followers disappeared into the sierra. He was nursing a profound rage at the United States, whom he believed had betrayed him. Villa had always preserved U.S. interests, protected U.S. property. He had had good relations with several U.S. Army officers, particularly General Hugh Scott. Why had they turned on him to help the hated Bearded One?

Betrayal on any level stoked the latent paranoia that stalked Villa the bandit's psyche. It drove him literally mad. He discovered that his old compañero Tomas Urbina had not only failed to rally to him at Celaya but had also absconded to his fortified hacienda with a horde of revolutionary gold. Villa was practically berserk in his fury. He and a picked force descended upon Urbina's hideout and slaughtered his followers. Yet, Villa couldn't make the call to execute his old friend. He sent him toward Chihuahua for medical treatment for the wounds he suffered in the assault.

Fierro shot him to pieces en route.

So…first old Tomas, now the Americans. Villa was beside himself with frustration, humiliation and rage. Come March of 1916, he would give vent to that rage in spectacular fashion. His target: the sleepy American border town of Columbus, New Mexico.

Francisco Villa's rage left him virtually unhinged. By the end of 1915, the vaunted Division del Norte had been swept away in a blood-red tide and his command had been reduced to a hard core of loyalists a rag-tag cadre of men and boys they conscripted at the muzzle of a gun.

Villa blamed the United States, which had recognized his hated rival Venustiano Carranza's faction as the legitimate government of Mexico and had materially assisted the Carrancistas in defeating the Division del Norte at the border city of Agua Prieta. The bandit in Villa knew only one way to quench his fury: He sought revenge.

In January 1916, a troop of Villistas led by the fanatically loyal Col. Pablo Lopez stopped a train near Santa Isabel, southwest of Chihuahua City. Aboard was a contingent of Americans, mostly mining engineers, who were on their way to reopen a silver mine that had closed down during the peak of the civil war.

Lopez ordered the Americans off the train, cursing and taunting them, telling them they ought to ask U.S. President

Woodrow Wilson for help, or perhaps appeal to Carranza for protection. He had them lined up on the tracks and detailed a couple of young Villistas to shoot them down with their Mausers.

It was a brutal scene. Many of the gringos who fell did not die at the first fire and were left writhing and screaming on the railroad bed. Lopez ordered a mercy shot, which his boys delivered at the muzzle of a Mauser pressed against the gringos' heads and blowing their brains out on the cinders.

Eighteen Americans were slain in what can only be described as a terrorist attack. The Wilson Administration didn't not act, reluctant to get embroiled in a confrontation with Mexico while the possibility existed that the U.S. would be pulled in to the Great War in Europe.

Within a few months, Villa would force Wilson's hand.

In the deepest dark of the morning of March 9, 1916, Villa and some four hundred and eighty five men slipped across the border and infiltrated the small burg of Columbus, New Mexico. It has never been determined with absolute certainty why Villa chose to attack Columbus. Perhaps he thought he could hijack arms from the U.S. forces stationed at nearby Camp Furlong, and the prospect of loot was certainly enticing to his wretched little army. It has been surmised that he also wanted revenge on a merchant named Sam Ravel who may have double-crossed him on an arms deal. Witnesses said that the Villistas searched for Ravel, inquiring after him by name and briefly taking hostage his young brother Arthur. Perhaps he was seeking to kill some Americans and provoke a U.S. invasion that would send patriotic Mexicans flocking to his tattered banner.

There are theories that German agents-provocateurs goaded Villa into an attack in order to get the U.S. tied down in Mexico. While there's no doubt that that was a strategic aim of the Germans, they seem to have been putting their bets on Carranza. There's no convincing evidence that the Columbus Raid was a German plot.

Whatever the strategic purpose, the attack on Columbus was a dismal failure. Ten civilians were killed and eight soldiers from Camp Furlong died repelling the attack. The defenders killed sixty seven Villistas in town, mostly after Lt. John Lucas and his men set up four French Benet-Mercie light machine guns and hosed down the streets — illuminated by fires set by the rampaging Villistas — with some 20,000 rounds of .30-06. Another hundred or so Villistas were slain as the fire-eating Col. Frank Tompkins pursued the retreating Villistas into Mexico.

Faced with an attack on U.S. soil, President Wilson had little recourse but to retaliate. He sent General John J. Pershing at the head of a Punitive Expedition to capture or kill Villa.

As with later strategic manhunts, the effort to track down an elusive enemy on his home ground proved futile. Despite hard campaigning, some close calls and the occasional skirmish that added to the Villista body count, the cavalry never quite caught up to Pancho Villa. Despite Carranza's grudging acceptance of their presence, U.S. troops got no cooperation and a good deal of hindrance from their Carrancista counterparts. In fact, the biggest battle during the whole campaign was a nasty scrap at the city of Carrizal, between American forces and Carrancista troops. Damn near sparked a real war with Mexico. The Germans must have been licking their chops.

But nobody other than the Kaiser's men wanted a war, so tensions ratcheted down. The Punitive Expedition pulled

back, and finally out of Mexico at the beginning of 1917 —
just in time for the U.S. to declare war on Germany and send
Pershing "Over There" at the head of the American Expedi-
tionary Force.

Villa came roaring back to life, aided in no small part by
Mexican resentment of the Yanqui invaders. For a while, Villa's revolutionary star was on the ascendant again. His forces
controlled most of the Chihuahuan countryside and he was
able occasionally to mount successful attacks on urban cen-
ters. He waged a savage war of reprisals with the Carrancista
general Pancho "The Rope" Murguia, notorious for dangling
captured Villistas from the trees lining the avenues of Chihuahua City.

Villa was no less savage. When the citizens of the town
of Namiquipa, once loyal, betrayed the location of an arms
cache, Villa retaliated by allowing his fighters to engage in
a mass rape of the town's women—something that he never
would have countenanced in his glory days as commander of
the Division del Norte.

Gradually, Villa's near-mad rage burned itself out. By
1920, Obregon and Carranza had fallen out and Obregon had
had Carranza turned out of power and then murdered. Villa
was willing to negotiate a truce.

He was granted a hacienda called Canutillo in the state
of Durango, where he maintained a substantial private bodyguard. A mellower Villa enjoyed developing a state-of-the-art
agricultural colony and spending time with his many children
by his many wives. The biggest conflict in his life was between
and among wives and mistresses. It drove the bandit chieftain
nearly crazy.

Old enmities finally caught up to him. Driving back
to Canutillo from a wedding in Parral in 1923, Villa was

ambushed and shot to bloody rags, along with several members of his personal staff.

The man who arranged and led the hit pleaded guilty—and served three months of a seven-year prison sentence. The fix was in, and the fixer was most likely Alvaro Obregon, el Presidente and the Last Man Standing in the Mexican Civil War. (He wouldn't stand forever though; in 1928, he was assassinated by a Catholic fanatic who was outraged at the anti-clerical Obregon's rough treatment of the Church. Shot five times in the face. They all went down hard).

Not long after his burial in Parral, someone — most likely a slippery American soldier of fortune named Emil Holmdahl broke into Villa's tomb and cut off his head. No one knows what became of the bandit's skull. Perhaps, as one legend has it, it served a rival general as an ashtray on his desk. Maybe, as many believe, it wound up in the collection of Yale's mysterious Skull & Bones fraternity. Just one more macabre twist in a dark tale.

Pancho Villa remains a restless borderland ghost, not a hero nor a villain, but a violent force of nature — the Fourth Horseman of the Mexican Apocalypse.

PART IV

SOUTH OF THE BORDER

*Never attach more feeling
to a thing than God does*

NO HABLO INGLÉS
By
MANUEL RAMOS

The lone ray of sunshine streaming through a crease in the dirt-stained window caught the corner of my eye and my head throbbed. A splinter of pain lodged itself in my eyeball. I sucked on a Tecate and a slice of lime whose rind had brown spots. I couldn't remember the name of the joint in Juárez that had produced the hangover.

"So, what's the deal, Manolo? Can you do any kind of lawyerin', or is it like, you know, over for good?"

Nick knew I didn't talk about my disbarment, but he asked crap all the time.

"Nick," I answered, looking him straight in his blood-shot eyes, "can you still say Mass? Give communion with the watered-down tequila you serve?"

He said something like "fuck you" and turned his attention to wiping the far side of the bar with a gray, stiff rag.

I dropped two bucks and eased out of the clammy, musty-smelling air of Nick's Cave and into the white glare and oven heat of another El Paso morning.

I hated the town, but that wasn't El Paso's fault. I hated myself and that meant I hated wherever I woke up. That summer it was El Paso.

I waited in the congestion and noise that led to the Santa Fe International Bridge, sweating through my shirt, as lost as if I'd been abandoned naked in the desert. I lit up my last American Spirit and crossed the street when the traffic slowed for a minute.

The diner was busy and I hesitated at the door until an old Mexican wearing a packing-house hardhat pushed himself from his table, stuck a few dollars under his fork, and walked out with a toothpick hanging from his lip. I took his place before it was cleared by the young Mexican busboy. He grimaced at me when he came to pick up the greasy plate and stained coffee cup but he didn't say anything. He also didn't wipe the crumbs off the tabletop.

I opened my notebook and stared at the pages of the great Chicano novel that I'd decided I would write that summer, seeing as how I didn't have much else to do. My words didn't make sense. Some of the sentences trailed off the edge of the page. I must've been drunk when I wrote most of them.

The waitress cleared her throat and I realized that she stood next to me.

"What you want, Manolo?" she asked in Spanish.

I answered, in English, "Eggs and chorizo, coffee. One of those grilled jalapeños."

She said, "Whatever," in English, and appeared to run away from me.

What the hell, I thought. We used to be friends. At least one night not that long ago we were really good friends. Why she act like that?

The door opened and hot air rushed in. I smelled sweat and grease.

"You the lawyer?" The accent was thick but the words were clear.

She was small, pretty, dark, and afraid.

"No, I'm not a lawyer."

"The man at the bar across the street." Her eyes were wide and her lips trembled. "He said the lawyer came in here and that he wore a white shirt. You're the only man in here with a white shirt."

I looked at the diner's other customers and she was right.

"But that doesn't make me a lawyer."

Tears welled up in her eyes but nothing rolled down her cheeks. She backed out of the diner, looked up and down the street, then raced in the direction of Mexico.

The frayed cuffs of my shirt had a thin border of dirt. I fingered the empty space where a missing button belonged.

The waitress appeared with my coffee. I stubbed out what was left of my smoke and carefully placed it in my shirt pocket. I said, "This used to be a very good shirt. I wore it in court. I used to kick butt in this shirt."

She rolled her eyes and shook her head.

"You are so full of shit, Manolo." She hurried away again.

I pulled out my wallet and was relieved to see the twenty. For an instant I thought I might have left it all in Juárez. I had more back in my room, in the so-called safe, but I understood that it was running out. The dregs of what I'd managed to salvage from the Colorado Supreme Court's order to reimburse my former clients couldn't last more than a few weeks.

I finished the breakfast, except for the chile, and drank several cups of coffee and finally left when the waitress stopped coming by. I crossed the street again and forced myself into Nick's.

Two men sat at the bar, dressed in cowboy hats and shirts, jeans and boots. They talked loudly with the speeded-up rhythm of Mexicans who lived too long on the American side of the border. I sat in one of the booths, almost in darkness. My eyes took their time adjusting to the change in light and when Nick asked me what I wanted, I could barely make out his silhouette.

"Just a beer. Tecate."

Nick kept a CD player behind the bar and I thought I heard Chalino Sánchez. The slightly off-key, high-pitched voice of the martyred wannabe filled the bar with a lament about bad luck with young women. An accordion, a tinny cymbal, brass horns and drums emphasized the singer's misery.

When Nick came back and set down the beer can, I grabbed his wrist.

"What that woman want, Nick? Why'd you send her to me?"

"The fuck I know? She said she was lookin' for the Chicano lawyer. There's only one asshole I know that fits that description. I told her you was across the street." He jerked his arm free of my grip.

"There are plenty of Chicano lawyers in this town. Too many. What made you think she wanted me?"

He'd turned away. He stopped, looked down at me. "She didn't have any money."

I rubbed my temples, took my time with the beer.

The two men at the bar stood up, arguing and shoving each other. Nick shouted at them to get the hell out but they ignored him. I squeezed myself into a corner of the booth and watched as one of the men pulled a knife from somewhere and.sliced his drinking pal. Drops of blood appeared on the slashed man's shirt. He slapped his chest with his left hand. Nick grabbed the man with the knife, knocked the weapon free, and wrestled him to the door. Curses and shouts filled the bar and whoever had followed

Chalino Sánchez on Nick's CD player was drowned out by the familiar sound of men fighting in a bar. The wounded man stumbled to the doorway just as Nick tossed out the knife-wielder.

The former friends stood about two feet apart, in the middle of the sidewalk. The cut man's fingers gripped his chest and were covered with blood. The other man grinned. He finally laughed and walked away. His bloody companion slowly followed.

"Look at this floor," Nick shouted. "Goddam blood spots. Now I got to get the bleach." His face was red and a thin line of blood traced his jawline.

I stood up from the booth and walked to where Nick examined the floor.

"That woman, Nick? What was her problem?"

"You fuckin' kiddin' me? Why didn't you ask her yourself? She said somethin' about her sister. Usual shit. Christ." He shook his head and disappeared into a closet. I heard him banging a bucket and shaking out a mop.

I made it back to my room and laid down on the bed. I sweated for an hour, listening to the traffic in the street below, smelling the traffic. I blotted out everything else about the room, the town, the day. When I decided to leave, I took off the white shirt and replaced it with a blue shirt that I had never worn in court.

I walked toward the border, to the bridge where anyone with a quarter can cross into Mexico unless the bridge is closed because of a bomb threat. There had been such a threat the day before and that had been my excuse to stay in Juárez longer than I had planned. That's what I had told myself at dawn when I tripped on the American side of the bridge and had trouble getting up.

I finished the butt saved from breakfast and scanned the line of people walking into Mexico. I looked over the vendors with their trinkets and gewgaws, tried to recognize the face of the small, dark, pretty, and frightened woman who had wanted to talk to a North American lawyer about her sister.

"You ever been to the shrine of Santa Muerte?" The boy asking the question had straight, thick hair, like some kind of Indian, and the darkest eyes I had ever seen on a human being. One of the eyes was crooked and it distracted me so that when he spoke I thought he was talking to someone behind and to the left of me.

"Saint Death? I don't think so. I don't have time, and I don't have any money."

"Hey, pocho, I don't want your money. I'm talking about La Santisima Muerte, the only real saint, the only one worth praying to anyway." His English was good, better than my Spanish, so we talked in English. "She only promises what she will actually deliver, and she treats everyone the same — rich, poor, Mexican, gringo."

The boy wasn't going anywhere so I asked a question. "What kind of shrine is this?"

"A special place. A girl got killed there and when her mother found the body it was covered in roses that bloomed for weeks after. Now people go there to ask for help."

"Why would I want to see this shrine?"

"You're looking for something. Ain't nothing she can't help find, because everything and everyone all end up with her anyway."

I used my handkerchief to wipe the sweat from the back of my neck. The monogrammed MT had faded from its original deep royal blue to a pallid gray. I stuffed the handkerchief back in my pocket.

"Tell me, boy. You think someone who is looking for a lost sister might go to the shrine?"

He smiled and exposed gaps in his teeth.

"She already has, pocho. About an hour ago. I took her myself."

"Show me." "Two American dollars."

"You said you didn't want money."

"That was before you wanted something."

I gave him the two bills and I thought how that could buy me a cold beer at Nick's.

The boy veered from the bridge and we dashed across the street. He scrambled into an alley, then another, turned back and headed to the outskirts of the town. I sweated like I had a fever, and my breath came hard and fast before we ended up in the basement of a broken-down apartment building.

We walked along a narrow concrete hallway that smelled of copal and marigolds. Candles lit the way into a dark, damp corner of the basement. Hundreds of candles. The boy kept walking, didn't look at me, didn't say a word.

The statute of the saint of death standing on a makeshift altar looked like the grim reaper to me. Various offerings surrounded it — food, money, photographs, pieces of clothing. About a dozen people kneeled around the altar and they mumbled prayers I couldn't understand. I walked around the small room and looked for the woman who'd confronted me in the diner but the only light came from candles and the people kept their faces down and hidden behind mantillas and dusty hats. I didn't see the woman.

I wanted to ask the boy to take me back but he was gone. Some in the crowd started to leave and I followed them down what I thought was the same candled hallway. They murmured to each other, stayed close and kept looking over their shoulders at me. They moved faster and I had to exert myself to keep up with them. They turned a corner but when I followed, they were gone. I was in another small room without candles, without any light. Spanish words and phrases and the brassy, loud grating music of a Mexican band bounced off the walls. Then words in a language I didn't recognize and music I'd never heard before floated through the hallway.

I waited. A few minutes passed, then another group of people from the shrine entered the room and shifted sharply to my left, toward an opening that I'd not seen.

I said, "Wait, show me the way. I'm lost."

An old woman wearing a black shawl over her waist-long gray hair stopped. She looked at me and said, "No hablo inglés."

I repeated my request in Spanish but she shrugged and trudged into the darkness. I followed the sounds of her footsteps. After a few minutes I heard nothing but I kept walking in the dark, sometimes feeling my way around corners, until I found myself in the stench and heat of a deserted El Paso alley.

An hour later I was back in Nick's, drinking a beer.

"They're on their way to lose their cherries, across the bridge." Nick smirked at the boys at the end of the bar. I assumed he talked to me because the underage boys were the only other people in the bar and he must have figured that he would be less susceptible to being shut down if he avoided them, even though he served them shots of tequila.

I didn't have a response.

"They found another one," Nick said.

"Another what," I asked, but I knew what he was talking about.

"A dead woman, out in the desert by the wire. Cut up like the others. Been missin' for weeks."

"How many's that?"

"There's no official count. Hundreds, thousands. Like that girl the woman was lookin' for. Missin' for weeks."

"How do you know that?"

He frowned. "She told me, what do you think? Anyway, she's lookin' for her missin' sister, in Juárez and El Paso. What the hell you think that means?"

I got up to leave. "Why would she want to talk to me about that? I can't do anything about her missing sister."

"Come on, Manolo. You can't do anything about anybody's problems. Remember? You screwed that up, as I heard you explain one night."

"Yeah, yeah. I screwed it up. So why would she want to talk to me?"

He shrugged, twisted his bar rag. "She heard about the American lawyer. That means somethin' to some people. She heard that the lawyer hung out in the bars. She tried to track you down. She thought you might be able to help, maybe you knew somebody, maybe you heard somethin'. She had nowhere else to go, no one else to talk to." He tossed his rag under the bar. "Dammit, Manolo, I don't know."

He walked over to the boys and said, "How about another one for the road?" They laughed uneasily and moved away when he tried to put his arm around the shoulders of the shortest kid.

I left Nick and his dingy bar and his ugly reputation and swore that I was done with all of it. I'd walked about two blocks when I saw her. She leaned against a brick wall, the side of a building that housed a mercado where every week tourists spent thousands of dollars on useless souvenirs and phony mementos.

She cringed when she saw me.

"I can't help. I don't know anything, anyone." I used my hands to emphasize my explanation.

She cocked her head. Her face was smudged with the salt of the tears that had finally flowed.

She reached into her thin jacket and waved a small gun. I shook my head and put my hands in front of me but she pulled the trigger. The shot made me jump, then I fell to the ground. The pain in my shoulder wrenched my torso. I twisted on the grimy sidewalk.

I gurgled one word: "What?"

"No hablo inglés," she said. She dropped the gun and walked away.

I sat up but dizziness bent me forward and I slumped to the sidewalk.

The hospital released me two days later. I left El Paso and returned to Denver.

When it snows my shoulder aches and I smell copal and marigolds.

THE WORK OF WOLVES
By
BRADLEY MASON HAMLIN

Devin blew a thick smoke ring from his Cuban, briefly capturing the full moon inside the ring before dissipating in front of the face of the man sitting across. He motioned to the moon across the table on the concrete terrace. "Good backdrop for the work of wolves, no?"

The man did not answer.

A holy man.

Preacher man.

A quiet man.

Devin thought about the confessional booth, must have been about six then, first time the good father reached inside his trousers.

"You know," he said, "I once asked a nun how the servants of the Lord could be so evil. She said, 'Little boy, we are all servants of God. You must have faith. Blind faith,' she said. Sure, a blind mind when the cleric says close the door." He smiled at his dinner companion. "Ain't that right, amigo?"

The man did not answer.

"But the question is," said Devin, "how do they sleep at night? Eh, how goes the sleep when the wolves howl?" As if in answer the hungry dogs below growled. "Me, I did not sleep so well. I thought when I got to Mexico City College, or as they call it now, Universidad de las Américas, I would be in paradise, away from the familia, away from the church, just good minds and good people."

Devin blew his smoke straight into the face of the man on the other side of the table, but still no response.

"I woke up screaming," he said.

Devin cut a hunk of panela with a cleaver and ate. "But I tried to worry away the terror with knowledge, knowledge of psychology, the philosophy of logic, and a whole lot of mescal, eh? Sí, I studied wickedness. I wanted to know why men are so goddamned evil."

He thought the man across gave a look with his eyes.

"What's a matter, don't like my language? I always wanted to walk into church and scream: Cock! Cock! Cocksucker! That's all you faggots want!"

Devin laughed.

"Yeah, I studied evil as if it were a math problem. I knew all the angles; knew all the angels. I wanted to unravel every myth until I could ..."

He took a drink of the vino rojo in front him and smiled. "Am I boring you?"

The man didn't answer.

"Well," said Devin, "no matter." He laughed again. "You have the right to remain silent.

"In the university, I read the crime novels; Cain, Chester Himes, and Hammett. Even read Mickey Spillane. Even though, most people don't care for Mickey anymore. Imagine that, millions once read the man, but now turn their backs on him, because he isn't 'literary.' You," said Devin, "won't turn your back on me, eh?"

Devin drank more wine.

"The readers prefer the lie. The window dressing. Prefer to pretend they're reading high art when all they want is the blood, the fucking, and the noise of the gun. At least Mickey told it true. Pulp is better than pretty paper. At times, I couldn't even take Chandler anymore. You could sense Chandler's fear, sense Chandler's fear of the cunt and the curves underneath the trench coat."

Devin stared at the preacher man. The man's expression did not change. "I decided to write my own stories. At least then the bad guys could really get fed to the wolves, no? Yes. Didn't have to dream up horrible crimes, either, did I? No."

Devin drank and considered that big fat moon hanging in the sky as his vision started to blur.

"In college," he said, "I drank tequila until I heard the skeletons laughing at my breakfast."

Devin reached over and put out his cigar on the forehead of the cleric.

"Everywhere I went I heard the bells of the church ringing like I was some kind of fucking monster, Quasimodo, no? The man with the invisible hunchback, carrying that weight around with me—listening to the laughter that comes from the first layer of skin and not the heart."

The cries of the dogs below rose with the moon climbing into the black night. Devin brushed aside the wine with his right arm, the glass and bottle smashing on the concrete. He grabbed the holy man up out of his seat and pulled him close. He could smell the fear, sweat, and the charred skin and blood from the cigar burn. The gag was wet and smelled like a puppy's chew rag. He dragged the kicking man over to the balcony. "Good thing I tied your hands, no? Yes, your hands are bad. Very very bad."

He lifted the man's arms from behind and forced the bound wrists up onto the balcony railing. You could hear a stifled scream of pain through the muffle. The man shook like a fish on a hook as Devin raised the meat cleaver. His arm chopped down fast, two times, and the hands fell to the barking dogs below.

This time you really could hear the scream.

Devin picked the man up and looked into his eyes. The blood was everywhere and the dogs made an incredible sound below, the sound of absolute hunger and desire.

Devin wanted to smile but couldn't. "To the dogs you go," he said.

Animals, he thought, listening to the dogs fight over the meat, they don't have free will. They just react to their environment or how people treat them.

Free will, he thought.

How people treat them, he thought.

Blind faith, he thought.

He pulled the pistol he had used to capture his prey and placed the weapon against his own temple.

Thought about it.

Mistake, he guessed.

Thinking ...

Free will then, he thought.

Simple.

Like a detective story, the answer always there.

Free will; not blind faith.

Devin put the pistol down.

God was tough, a real hardboiled egg.

He again considered that moon hanging up there in the sky. He considered the hot breeze against his skin. He could smell the Mexican palm trees. There was life, out there, somewhere. He could hear the dogs barking, growling, chewing, and eating. If nothing else, the dogs seemed pleased.

*The creative person should have
no other biography
than his works.*
— B. Traven

The argument can be made Borderland Noir truly started in the literary sense with the 1927 novel, *The Treasure of the Sierra Madre*, penned by the enigmatic author B. Traven. The shadowy novelist may or may not have actually been a German actor-turned-anarchist named Ret Marut whose convictions and politics set him on a desperate and enduring international scramble. Whoever he really was, Traven detested capitalism, embraced obscurity outside the publication of his works and likely died a shady octogenarian in Mexico City in the late 1960s. Novelist Martín Solares explores the Traven mystery in this excerpt from his highly-recommended novel, *The Black Minutes* (English translation by Aura Estrada and John Pluecker).
—CM

TRAVEN

(Excerpted from *The Black Minutes*)

By

MARTÍN SOLARES

Get one thing straight: as long as you're in this business, you're not going to have any friends. You heard right: not one friend. Everyone who gets close to you is going to ask for something or want to use you for something. You can't trust anybody. A police officer doesn't have friends when he's doing his job; a police officer only has enemies. The trick is to learn how to avoid them.

Don't tell anybody where you live and never open your door in one fell swoop, just in case they're messing with you. If you eat out for lunch, look for a seat where they can't surprise you (the doors, keep an eye on the doors), and if you have to be next to a window, close the curtain or lower the light, so they won't be able to shoot at you from the outside.

Don't drink too much, don't take drugs, don't go into a dark place unarmed, don't make deals with people from that world (the criminal world, I mean, but don't make deals with your coworkers, either, just in case one day they get sick of you and want to get rid of you), and like the santeros say, put a glass of water next to your bed every night and pray to Saint Judas Martyr; just in case your soul gets thirsty, you don't want it to head off looking for a drink and never come back.

One day, years ago, Rangel and his uncle had just got back from making an arrest, when Lolita called them aside. "Lieutenant, a man came to look for you. It was an older gentleman, about eighty years old. He left you a book."

His uncle's face lit up. "Look at that, what good news!"

Don Miguel smiled big and showed the book to Rangel. It was copy of *The Treasure of the Sierra Madre*, dedicated *To my good friend, Don Miguel Rivera*. And it was signed *T*, just like that, all alone on the page, like a cross.

"A man about eighty years old, leather jacket and a straw hat?"

"Yeah. He said he was staying in the same place as always."

The old man nodded his head and went to make a phone call. Twenty minutes later he asked his nephew, "You got a lot of work right now?"

"The usual."

"Drop what you're doing and meet me at the bar in the hotel Inglaterra at two."

At two o'clock on the dot, Rangel met his uncle at one of the tables in the middle of the bar. A man with graying hair was at his side, a straw-colored hat on the seat next to him.

"Vicente," his uncle said, "I'd like to introduce Mr. Traven Torsvan, a writer."

They ate lunch at a restaurant on the riverbank: a few giant shrimp; an oyster, octopus and ceviche cocktail; a little cheese tortillas; and a house specialty: crabs à la Frank (crab meat with cheese and a magnificent olive oil). During the lunch, Mr. Torsvan took out a copy of *The Death Ship* and signed it for Rangel.

"You don't see the waiter, do you?"

"No."

"He hasn't been paying any attention to us. If you see him, wave him over."

But the waiter was nowhere to be seen.

"Where do you live?"

"On the other side of river. Near the dock."

"Near the Williams hacienda?"

"Right next door, in the foreman's house."

"And you know what they say about that house? I'll you the story while we wait to order."

As you know, the Williams family came from Germany, escaping from the First World War. They settled all along the coast and their largest property, their hacienda, started here in Paracuán and extended all the way to the Cerro del Nagual: as far as the eye can see. The oldest son, who was a bum, a drinker, and a womanizer, went to live in Haiti. When his father died, he returned to run the hacienda. He did it for a month, but soon his employees started to die. An animal was eating them in the forest, a tiger. It was hunting them down. It was so strong it could carry a man in his jaws and eat him up in a tree where no one could stop him. Bullets didn't affect him, even if the rifle had been blessed.

One of the few men who survived an encounter with the tiger spread the rumor that the animal looked like the young Mr. Williams and even had the same eyes. After that point, no one wanted to go near the hacienda. It seemed that the employees killed were those who had worked closest to Mr. Williams in the past few weeks. Some people said it was the ghost of the old man, that his son had cast a spell on him and forced him to wander around like a lost soul. Others thought it was the son himself. In any case, the animal was going to eat them one by one. They tried to kill it with silver-tipped bullets but no marksman could shoot it; the tiger was always too quick for them. The ones who wanted to leave and go somewhere else found themselves locked in by huge iron fences and guards preventing their escape: they had signed a contract and they had to work on the ranch until the end of the year.

Soon they realized the animal attacked on a schedule, once every thirty days. It attacked once and then relaxed for three weeks. Each time it made its monthly kill, the survivors would breathe easier; they had another three weeks to live.

Five months later, it was the turn of the poorest family on the ranch. Mr. Williams went to visit them and said one of them was to go into the depths of the forest to guard the harvest. The oldest brother excused himself, because he had four children; the second brother did the same, because his wife was expecting twins; and the third, who was said to be incredibly brave, was terrified and burst into tears. Then the youngest in the family asked for them to let him go. He was named Jacinto and he was fifteen years old; everyone loved the boy. Perfect, said Mr. Williams, and he left.

When Mr. Williams' niece found out, the girl, who had been Jacinto's playmate, went to the see the boy and gave him a packet with a word of advice. The boy didn't doubt the girl's sincerity, but he asked himself, What if the others got the same advice? Unlike his friends, he didn't take a rifle with him into the jungle, just a few chickens and the girl's packet. When night fell, he made a fire and started to make an exquisite dinner. When it was so dark he couldn't see beyond the fire, he heard something close by, stepping on some twigs. He stood up, grasping a picture of the Virgin Mary. And the tiger showed up. Just as people said, the animal was huge and horrific, more than six feet long. It had claws the size of knives instead of hands. Its tail was as thick as an elephant's trunk, and it had long whiskers. Its hair was blond with black stripes. Its eyes were green. And it smiled, its tongue hanging out of its mouth. The animal came up and said, "Good evening, may I sit down?"

"Of course," said Jacinto, "please take a seat, sir."

"Whatever you're cooking smells great. What is it?"

"Chicken with boiled cabbage."

"Ah, sauerkraut. And those bottles you're chilling, what are they?"

"Riesling wine."

"Riesling wine from Germany! It's been a long time since I ate sauerkraut and drank Riesling wine. And it's my favorite dish. Are you going to ask me to eat with you?"

"Yes, sir. All of this is for you."

"OK," the tiger said, "but don't think I'm going to spare your life. I'll eat the sauerkraut and the chickens, and afterward I'll have you for dinner as well."

"As you wish, sir." And Jacinto rushed to pour the wine.

After taking the first bite, the tiger said something had hurt, maybe there was a stone in the food. "It must have been a chicken bone," said Jacinto, and the animal took another bite, licking its whiskers. After finishing the first chicken, the beast asked Jacinto for the second. Then it ate the third and the fourth. The fifth one was eaten directly from the pot. As the beast ate, Jacinto served the first, the second, and finally the third bottle of wine. As it drank, the animal was getting happier and happier, and it roared in between bites. When Jacinto served the second bottle, it was talking to itself and singing in German. When he poured the third bottle, the animal scratched his arm. When it had finished the last chicken, it threw the pot and shouted, "The appetizers were good, but now it's time for dinner!" The animal stood up and, taking its first step toward Jacinto, slipped and fell. Jacinto took advantage of the animal's being too drunk to escape.

Everyone was surprised to see Jacinto come back. And they were even more surprised to see the young Mr. Williams fall ill that same day. First, they said, "He woke up with a headache." And then: "He's sick; he ate something that made him sick. "The foreman, another German, went to ask Jacinto if he had run into an animal in the forest. Jacinto said no. "Are you sure you didn't see anything?" Jacinto was positive.

The second day, the foreman went to ask if he hadn't seen a tiger or something like that. "And you didn't notice if that animal hurt itself somehow?"

"No," said Jacinto. "I didn't see anything."

The third day, Mr. Williams died. The doctor who examined him said there were five silver bullets in his body. "One perfectly hidden in each chicken," said Jacinto.

From then on, the workers didn't have any other problems. Jacinto married the old man's niece and they founded a soda company, Cola Drinks. That's why the Williamses are dark-skinned with light-colored eyes.

"Ah," Mr. Torsvan concluded, "finally the waiter is here. What are you going to have?"

After lunch they drank a bottle of whiskey, then coffee.

"Why don't you take us to visit your mansion, Vicente?" his uncle suggested. "You can see the dock from there. Besides, it's not far from here."

They bought a bottle of cognac and Mr. Torsvan handed a cigar to each of them. Since the old men wanted to see the ships, Rangel set them up in rocking chairs on the terrace, so they would be able to talk at ease. The breeze coming off the river scared away the mosquitoes and made the heat more bearable.

The sun descended slowly in the sky, lighting up the other side of the river. Don Miguel Rivera was happy. "In the twenties, you could see javelinas and deer drinking from the river. Do you remember?" he asked the German. "You lived around here."

"Yes," he replied.

"You had to kick them to scare them away."

Ah, Uncle Miguel, Vicente thought to himself. He'd never seen him so happy. Obviously he was happy to run into his buddy. Half an hour later, Don Miguel Rivera poured the last glass and confessed, "Vicente, I'm thinking of retiring."

"Really, why?"

"It's about that time."

"No way. What are you talking about?"

"Wait a second, let me speak. As I was saying to you, I've been in this job forty years, and the other day I really started to think."

He was referring to something that had happened recently. Eight days before, while they were chasing a thief on the docks, Rangel had noticed that his uncle was short of breath, so he parked the patrol car and let the suspect go. "It's over," the old man said. "You had that asshole."

"Don't worry, Uncle, your health is the most important thing." And they went to see Dr. Ridaura.

"It's been forty years. Besides, I hadn't told you, but there's a killer on my tracks."

"What!" Rangel shouted. "You should have told me, tío. Tell me now, and I'll go look for him."

"They call him *the silent killer*. And when that killer's after you, there's no reason to take any risks."

"No, don't get ahead of yourself, tío. We'll look for him and put him in his fucking place. Besides, if you retire, I retire, too. What am I going to do by myself?"

"If you like it, keep at it. I think you're made for this. How long have you been working, a year?"

"A year and a half."

"That's right. When I retire, I'm going to leave my pistol to you, to help keep you out of trouble."

"Yeah, but don't say that. You've got a long time till retirement."

"We'll see."

"The first ones your uncle arrested," said Mr. Torsvan, "were Cain and Abel."

"Look, skipper, you can't say anything; you've got ten years on me."

"That's why you should show some respect."

"If you're so respectable, why don't you write anymore?"

"Of course I'm writing. I just finished a novel for children. It's story of a woodcutter who gets lost in the jungle. A run-in with God, the devil, and death."

"It's all fairy tales. Why don't you write something more realistic, something more serious, more worthy of you? That story about the woodcutter has been told a thousand times!"

"You want a serious story, Vicente? I'll tell you the story of a police officer who let a guy with no papers go in the thirties."

Rangel thought, What are they talking about?

"You know, your uncle knew who B. Traven was and didn't turn him in. All around the world, the press would have paid to find out who Traven really was. Even though uncle knew, he let him go. A long time after that, when Dr. Quiroz Cuarón discovered Traven's identity, he boasted about being the best detective in the world. I had to tell him: But you aren't, Dr. Quiroz. The first one to find out was Don Miguel Rivera in the port of Paracuán, more than thirty years ago."

"More than forty," said his uncle.

"Who's telling this story, you or me?"

"Well, if you're going to tell that one again, you'll have to forgive me but I'm going to go lie down. Will that hammock hold me, Vicente?"

"Yeah, go right ahead."

His uncle stood up. "Excuse me, skipper," he put his hand on the older man's shoulder. "This officer is retiring from circulation."

"Go and relax, you deserve it at your age."

His uncle laughed loudly and patted his friend on the shoulder, then headed off to the hammock.

Torsvan sang a few verses in a foreign tongue, which made Rangel's ears perk up. "Excuse me, sir, where are you from? Are you German?"

"What, you don't understand me when I speak Spanish? Is my pronunciation that bad?"

"Of course not, your Spanish is very good."

"Then I'm Mexican."

And since he could see Rangel was surprised, he told his story.

"I came to Tampico in 1929. I got here in the cargo ship *Alabama*, with no money and no papers. They had kicked me out of three countries. I was in the Alps, between France, Belgium and Holland. At that moment, they were kicking me out of Belgium, so I considered my options. If I went to Holland, the sentence for traveling without papers was six months in a nasty prison, sharing a cell with a lot of shady characters with bad food and the chill of the cold night. That was the punishment in Holland. In Belgium, it was eight months, but I knew the Belgian police were looking to give me a good beating if I went back to cross the border again. If I waited for my escort to leave me and went back to Belgium, most likely they'd still be waiting for me, and before locking me up for six months with only bread and water, they'd torture me; those border guards were a mean lot. If I returned to France, they would sentence me to ten months in jail, but I'd be well fed, with decent food and a blanket. So I went to France. After they kicked me out of Spain, I went to Portugal and then to Mexico, as I already told you. I loved between Tampico and Paracuán, and then in Acapulco and Chiapas.

"I met your uncle in 'twenty-nine. I was able to avoid deportation that year. Someone who wanted to do me harm reported me as illegally in the country. The average cop would have taken advantage of my situation, but your uncle came to interrogate me, understood my case, and didn't bother me again. Curious, no? I've only told the story of this part of my life twice, and both times Lieutenant Rivera was present. I'd say the circle is closing, wouldn't you?

"Imagine it's 1928, a little before the Great Depression. Imagine a young German playwright — handsome, strong, intelligent—and imagine an actor. Do you know who Peter Lorre is? No? It's not really important, but he was one of his best friends. The playwright is becoming very popular. At that point in his life they are mounting his third production in Germany, and people wait in long lines to get in to see it. Offers from producers rain down; he has to push actresses away, everyone wants to work with him. His girlfriend is one of the most well-known blondes of the stage. They swore their eternal love for each other, and he's thinking of writing a drama so she can play the lead.

"One day at the end of the play they tell him a producer wants to meet him. Usually, the playwright would not have seen him, since those matters were his agent's responsibility, but the playwright was about to have a birthday and thought it was a joke by the owner of the theater. So he received the visitor in his girlfriend's dressing room, and instead of the ostentatious millionaire he was used to dealing with, he found three men dressed with a marked simplicity; they hadn't polished their shoes and one of them had a suit with patches on it. From the start of the conversation, the playwright behaved as if her were playing a role, and that was his error; it's enough to fake your belief in something to make that something become reality.

"The playwright asked in an exaggerated tone: 'What can I do for you, gentlemen?'

"'Mr. Torsvan, I presume? A pleasure. We are Misters Le Rouge, Le Jaune, and Le Noir.'

"'I guess they're fake names.' The playwright was pleased with the apparent joke.

"The one who seemed the most together says to him, 'They told us to come and see your work and we weren't disappointed. We enjoyed it quite a bit, and we'd like to make you an offer.'

"The playwright appreciates the kind words but doesn't know how to respond. These guys want to hire him? How are they going to pay him? Do they really not know how much he charges? They ask him if he thinks the same way as the play's main character and he explains to them that the author always identifies with his characters, but that in this play in particular, his favorite character is indeed the young idealistic lawyer who defends the poor. They playwright notices them nudging each other, and they decide to continue. They ask him very intelligent questions about the background of his stories, very honest questions like simple people ask.

"With his interest piqued, he asks them what their offer is all about. They look at one another, and one of them sticks his hand in his suit jacket and hands him a paper. When he unrolls it, be notices the poster is printed in red ink, with a hammer and a sickle. They were members of the German Communist Party, which at the time was underground. They defended the workers, organized resistance groups, and wanted to build unions, and that was why their lives were in danger.

"'You haven't realized it, but your plays have a lot in common with our struggle. We want to hire you to write a play for us.'

'Yes, the other visitor added, your new play could change a lot of lives.'

"'Change lives? That's not my project,' the playwright argued. 'I'm looking for other things. Besides, a writer requires a certain comfortable environment to write peacefully.' He thought this was going to scare them off, but one of them, wearing worn-out shoes, stepped forward and offered him an envelope. The playwright opened it and looked through its contents. 'Ha, you must be joking. I'm very sorry, but it's too little. I spend this in a weekend!'

"'What for some is very little, for others represents a lot of work,' they told him. 'Thirty of our most dedicated comrades worked extra hours for months to collect that money. It represents the sweat and toil of three dozen workers.'

"The playwright stutters. He says he already had deals for his next two plays and he doesn't have time to write one on request, but they insist. They tell him that his play is going to be important, it's going to change many people's lives, and he has to write it. To clear up any doubt, they invited him to attend one of their clandestine gatherings. When? Right now. Always looking for new subjects, he accepts the invitation and leaves the envelop on his girlfriend's dressing table, hidden behind a number of actors' photos and bottles of makeup.

"OK, so as not to draw the story out, he ends up accepting. What he sees in the meetings moves him and reveals a part of the world he didn't know about until then. Inconceivable stories for a civilized country, incredible injustice, regions of suffering he should have known about. So he drops everything and sets to work on that play, he helps mount the production, and he even participates in the rehearsals. A week before the opening, there's an important meeting. The playwright attends the meeting with his actors, but they're attacked by the police and many are shot. They take him for dead and throw him in the truck with the other bodies. He saves himself from being killed, because he jumps out of the truck as soon as it starts up.

"He crosses the border into France; he's illegal in five countries in Europe. Finally, he's able to board a ship in Portugal and get to the United States, but they don't let him in. He takes the cargo ship *Alabama* and gets off in the Gulf of Mexico.

"He gets to a town, Tampico: What a town! Afterward he moves to Paracuán. He sends a letter to his girlfriend using a false name. He tells her what happened and asks for her help. With the money he earned on the ship, he rents a little room on the docks and waits, but the money disappears quickly. He has to do any and every job just to make it as an illegal. He becomes a stevedore on the docks, a delivery man in the market, a worker in the oil wells. A hard, hard life! He lives in horrible rooming houses on flea-ridden cots, sharing a room with twenty other people. When there's no work, he begs for money from foreigners. He ends up fighting over a cigarette butt with other bums.

"Every Friday, he goes to check the mail to see if he got a letter. There is no response for months. Once, he gets a contract to work in the most remote of the oil wells. He has to work fourteen hours under the relentless sun, in a place where tigers are heard roaring at night. He's there for two months. He loses more than twenty pounds.

"When he gets back from the oil well, they tell him he got a telegram from the United States. The playwright almost tears up the envelope, he's so excited. The letter is from his girlfriend, who was able to leave the country and is living in New York. She doesn't give any address. If you are alive, she writes, send a letter to this post box. A week later, she sends him a money order for two hundred dollars (a fortune for someone who doesn't have a cent) and asks him to wait for her in Tampico at the Hotel Inglaterra.

"He goes to the barber shop, buys a new outfit, lives in a cheap but more respectable hostel than the ones he used previously, and a week before his girlfriend arrives, he moves to the designated hotel. The white room seems huge and empty to him. He knows that everything is OK, but as the days pass, he is overtaken with doubt: *Why didn't she tell me to meet her at the border? Why didn't she tell me to meet her in New York? Why couldn't she drop everything and come look for me?*

"When she finally arrives, the playwright goes to meet her at the docks. They hug for a long time, and she tells him that he can't go back to Germany. Officially, he is said to be dead, but the police are waiting to kill him. They read his Communist play and know he supported the organization. 'This has to be very clear,' she says, 'You can't go back. They know you're alive. They're looking for you to kill you.'

"He tells her he doesn't care; the best thing is that she has found him and finally they are going to be together again. 'Oh, Torsvan,' the girls explains. 'I have to tell you something,' and she pulls loose from his arms. While he was in jail in France, she met a movie director, a Mr. Lang, and they were married. 'Understand, we thought you were dead. I'm at the prime of my life, it was a huge opportunity. We don't have a future together. The best thing would be for you to stay in this country and forget about me.' He doesn't respond, but goes out onto the balcony for a cigarette, watching the ships take up their anchors and set out from the docks. He stays there for a long time, even though she calls for him from inside. He realizes the Communists were right; his play changed at least one life — his own.

"He decides to turn his life around. Back inside, he asks his girlfriend, 'And the money? Were you able to take out my savings?'

"'I'm sorry, Torsvan. They canceled your accounts; the only thing I could recover was this. Do you want me to lend you money? No? Then take this.' And she hands him the envelope he left in her dressing room, the envelope from the three Communists. What a paradox! He, who used to spend that amount in a weekend, is now forced to make it last for a while.

"When she leaves, he decides to grow his own food. In all, he lives for a year on the money from the envelope. He buys the basics to hunt and plant crops and he goes to the country, between Tampico and Paracuán. He rents half the fields from an Indian. He lives in a wood hut, where there are scorpions as big as his hand. Every morning, he takes an insect out of his shoes. To get water, he has to walk almost two miles. He writes a novel about living like that — really, autobiography disguised as fiction — in which he tells the story of his escape from Germany. Then he writes to others about his experiences in the jungle. There comes a time when he decides to do something with them, and, using a pseudonym, he sends them to his former theatrical agent. He knows he's playing with fire and this could cost him his life, but despite it all he signs with his mother's maiden name, that almost no one knows, and instead of his first name he uses the single letter B. Inventing that initial, he thinks it through like this: until they killed me, I lived on the A side of my life; now I'm on the B side.

"His agent responds with an enthusiastic letter, saying that he likes the books but that he only works with plays, but B. Traven insists: They have spoken very highly of you; they say you are an honest person. The agent doesn't promise anything but tells him he will try.

"A year and a half later, the writer receives another telegram. He has a contract for his first novel. A year later, it's a bestseller in Europe. He sells a hundred thousand copies in the United States. There's an offer to make a movie out of the third novel; they want John Huston to direct. He gets mountains of letters, and the most frequent comment is: Your novel has changed my life. At that moment, the author says, I don't understand anything anymore, and he moves to Mexico City."

Mr. Torsvan doesn't say another word. Rangel takes the chance to ask, "Do you think a person like me could find his path again?"

To respond, the writer takes out an old gold coin, a heavy little German mark shimmering in the afternoon light.

"Are we, each of us, just one person or are we inhabited by a multitude?"

And he handed him the coin. Rangel took another sip from his drink. It was a splendid afternoon, and his uncle was missing it! So he decided to wake him.

"Tío," he said.

But Miguel Rivera Gonzáles didn't answer. He had died in his sleep, after smoking a cigar and drinking half a bottle with his friends.

Since they didn't know what to do, they called Dr. Ridaura, who came and took his pulse and placed a mirror under his nose, but it didn't steam up.

"The silent killer," she said, and since the others gave no sign of understanding, she added, "That's what they call high blood pressure. It kills quickly and leaves no trace. One day you're healthy and the next day, *bam!* Believe me, I'm so sorry. He was a good person."

They buried him on Friday afternoon. In attendance were Mr. Torsvan, the mayor at the time, all his police coworkers, from the night watchman to the chief, and, a little removed from the crowd, two dozen residents of the Colonia Coralillo.

Three days later, still grieving, Rangel had to go up to the wreck of a place where his uncle had lived to gather up his personal effects. His ex-wife kept the money in his bank account, which she was supposed to distribute to the kids, and Rangel took away the rest. He kept a picture of his uncle and Mr. Torsvan and some other people. If Rangel had some knowledge of the movie world, he would have known that those individuals were Humphrey Bogart and John Houston, and that the picture was taken during the filming of *The Treasure of the Sierra Madre* in the port of Tampico ... but Rangel wasn't an educated guy.

To his surprise, he found four records: Los Panchos' *15 Hits*, *Supersonico* by Ray Conniff, Vivaldi's *Four Seasons*, and Frank Sinatra's *Something Stupid*: his uncle was eclectic. Without saying a word, he piled up the suits, the ties, the white shirts, the shoes and the jackets that he was going to throw out. He only kept two things: the thirty-eight caliber Colt and the shoulder holster.

FERRYMAN

By

JAMES SALLIS

L et me say this: I'd stopped dating, stopped looking, stopped even fantasizing that the sexy young woman with tattoos at the local 7-Eleven where I bought my beer was going to follow me home. Still felt a gnawing loneliness, though, one that never quite went away and drew me out again and again, till I had a regular round of watering holes, places that exist outside the official version, largely unseen even by those who live near, part of the invisible city. Clinica Dental, for instance.

On any given day there you look out windows to see saguaro that grow for seventy five to one hundred years before the first arm comes along, and inside to see ninety nine percent Hispanic faces. Color and facial features ambiguous, Spanish serviceable as long as things stay simple, I don't stand out. And I'm not there for free dental care, which makes it easier, I'm just there to be in the flow, to climb out of my own head and place in the world for a look around.

Airports, bus stations, parks — all are great for that. But county hospitals and free clinics may be the best.

After a while I began to feel that I wasn't alone, that someone shared my folly. Like me, she blended in, but by the third or fourth glance, cracks started to show. Patients came and went — maids in uniform, yard workers, mothers with multiple kids in tow, an old guy that weighed all of eighty pounds lugging a string bass – and neither of us budged. From time to time, reading one of those self-help, motivational books with titles like *Find Happy* or *Say Yes to Your Dream* that turn out to be warmed-over common sense, she'd look up and smile. Now, of course, I understand book and visit for what they were: advanced research in how to pass.

When she left, I followed her on foot crosstown to Hava Java and lingered outside as she ordered. The place was busy, a jumble of young and old, hip and straight, some with lists of beverages to take back to the office, so she had a longish wait before staking out a table near the side window.

Two cups. Meeting someone, then.

But as I started to turn away, she beckoned, pointing to the second cup. I went in and sat. The kind of steel chair that looks great on paper but fits no part of the human body — legs too short, back at the wrong angle, seat guaranteed to find and grind bones. A young woman, evidently mute, went from table to table carrying a cardboard sign.

PLEASE HELP
HOMELESS
SPARE CHANGE?

When my table mate held out a ten-dollar bill, their eyes met for half a beat before the woman took it, bowed her head, and moved away.

"Es café solo," my companion said, gesturing to the cup before me, "espero que esté bien."

Given my skin color and where we just were, a fair assumption. "Perfect," I said.

Seamlessly she shifted to English. No taint of accent in her voice. She could easily have been from the Midwest, from Washington state, l.c, from California. I noted the lack of customary accoutrements. No purse or backpack, no tablet, no cell phone in its holster. Just the book and a wallet with, presumably, money and ID. I noted also how closely she observed everything: figures passing in the world outside, the low buzz escaped from earphones at a table close by, a couple leaning wordlessly in towards one another. Had I ever known someone so content to let silence have its place, someone uncompelled to fill every available space with sound?

Natalie was like that. Three or four weeks after we got together we'd planned a weekend trip to El Paso and she came out of the house that morning at six, smell of new citrus in the air, with a backpack you could get a small lunch and maybe a pair of underwear in.

"That's it?" I said.

"Like to stay light on my feet. You?"

My now-shamed suitcase was in the trunk.

Light eased itself gingerly above the horizon as we moved through Natalie's battered neighborhood. The first three entrances onto I-10 were jammed. The city had grown too fast — a six-foot man on a child's playhouse chair. Too many bodies shipping in from elsewhere, riding the wagons of their dreams westward, northward.

This was the girlfriend who told me I didn't communicate, that I shut myself off from everyone and, when I shrugged, said, "See?" But that was later. Of the trip mostly what I remember is driving along the river one evening on our way to dinner and the best chile relleno I ever had, looking over at shanties clustered on the bluff above and thinking how could anyone possibly expect that these people wouldn't try to cross over? Deliverance was right here, so easily visible, scant yards away. Reach out and you could touch it.

On that same trip, walking to breakfast the next morning, we found the bird's nest. I turned to say something and Natalie wasn't there. Two or three steps back, she was down on both knees.

"It must have fallen out. From up there." She pointed to a palo verde. "There's one broken egg shell."

She was almost to the point of tears as she picked the nest up, ran a finger gently along it. Twigs, pieces of vine, what looked to be string or twine, silvery stuff, grass or leaves.

"There's something here with words on it." She held the nest close to her face. "Can't make them out."

Across the street stood a Chinese restaurant, alley running alongside, Dumpsters at the rear. I walked back for a better look at the nest. What she was seeing, intertwined among the twigs and other detritus, were slips from fortune cookies.

That's also when I found out what Natalie read since, as it turned out, the backpack held more books than clothing. When she moved in not long after, she brought a sack of jeans and T-shirts, ten stackable plastic bookshelves, two dozen boxes of science fiction paperbacks, and little else. Kuttner, Sturgeon, Emshwiller, Heinlein, Delany, Russ, LeGuin. I'd begun picking up the books she forever left behind in the bathroom, on the kitchen table, splayed open on counters, in the fissure between our shoved-together twin beds. Many had been read and reread so many times that you had to hold in pages as you made your way through. Before I knew it, I was hooked.

The books were all she took when she moved out, that and her favorite photo, a panoramic shot of the Sonoran desert looking unearthly, lunar, forsakenly beautiful. Over the years I'd searched out copies of some of the books at Changing Hands and Bookmans. For the panorama I had only to drive a few miles outside the city bubble.

Not having been theretofore of an analytical turn of mind, nonetheless I came to recognize that, fulfilling as were these fantastic adventures in and of themselves, something far more substantial moved restless and reaching beneath the surface. The Creature swam in dark reverse of the woman in her white bathing suit above. Unsuspected worlds co-exist just out of frame and focus with our own. Transformations are a commonplace.

The same transformations occur in memory, I know, and what I now recall is the two of us standing there looking at the bare expanse together. Natalie's photo of the Sonoran desert, or the closest I could find to it — but it's her, my new brief companion, speaking.

"It looks as though it doesn't belong to this world."

"I often think that."

"Beautiful."

"Yes."

She moved closer. Our arms touched. Her skin was cold.

"Whatever lived there, on that world, its life would be spent in the pursuit of water. Certain plants would harbor water, water that could be harvested. When the blue moon came, always unpredictably, it would bring sudden, rapid rains. For an hour, two hours before they evaporated, shallow pools would form. And hundreds of life forms would race towards those pools, fill them, congest them. They would overflow."

"That's quite a story — put together from almost nothing."

"Isn't that how we understand the world we find ourselves in, by stitching together bits and pieces of what we see?"

As we had climbed stairs to the apartment she asked what I did for a living and I explained that I worked here at home, nothing of great interest really, pretty much the high-tech equivalent of filing, staring at computer screens all day. How living all the time in your head can make you strange. That getting out among others on a regular basis helped. We'd wandered towards the computer as we talked. The desert photo was my screen saver.

I'd drawn the blinds partly closed when we entered. Sunlight slipped through them at an angle and fell in a rectangle on the desk, looking like a second, brighter screen.

"Eventually," she went on, "one species wins out in the race for water. For space and food. Drives the rest away or destroys them. But without them, without those others keeping the balance, that species can't survive. It crosses over, into a new land. It changes."

"And as with all immigrants, now everything becomes about fitting in, being invisible."

Quiet for a moment, she then said, "Becoming. Yes, exactly. It finds a way to go on."

Later I will remember Apollinaire, my mother's favorite poet: Their hearts are like doors, always doing business. I'll remember what Garrett, a friend far more given to physicality than I, wrote in one of his stories, describing intercourse: We were bears pounding salmon on rocks. And I will remember her face above me in early dawn telling me I would never be alone again.

Then she died.

I remember…

Within minutes there's a knock at the door. Dazed, I open it to find a man who looks exactly like her. There are others with him, a man and a woman who look the same. They come in, roll her body in bedspread and blanket Cleopatra-style, bear her away.

"Thank you," one of them says as they leave.

That morning I go for a long walk along the canal. I take little note of the water's slow crawl, of those who pass and pace me, of traffic on the interstate nearby, of the family of ducks who've made this their improbable home. I cannot say what I am feeling. Heartbreak. Shock. Pain. Loss. And at the same time…

Happiness, I suppose. Contentment.

Two weeks later I'm walking down the street on my way to coffee, peering up into trees for possible nests, when I hear the voice in my head. "Nice day," it says. "Maybe we could go for a walk along the canal later."

I've come to a stop with the first words, looking around, wondering about this voice, what's going on here — but of course I know. A father always knows. I was bringing a new life across.

CORRIDA DE TOROS
By
SAM HAWKEN

He waited in the motel, cut off from daylight by heavy, plastic-lined curtains. He kept a gun on the nightstand and watched free satellite TV with the sound turned off. When he was hungry, he crossed the gravel parking lot and two lanes of backwater farm road to a small gas station. He paid cash for junk food, beer, and cigarettes. He made no small talk with the acne-spattered teenager who worked the counter.

He got into a rhythm with the woman who cleaned the rooms: she rolled her cart up to the door, knocked twice, and he opened up long enough to swap dirty sheets and towels for clean ones. He never asked to have the bathtub or toilet scrubbed out.

There was little traffic past the motel, and he liked it that way. Whenever tires crunched in the parking lot, he tensed up. He grabbed the pistol and crept to the drapes to peek out. Despite the late-summer heat, he didn't run the air conditioner; he didn't want the noise to cover any other sound.

He slept lightly. He washed his clothes in the bathroom sink and hung them to dry in the tub. Every other day he shaved. His hair had once been short, but was going long from neglect. From time to time, he ran his fingers over his scalp, his expression rueful. He was, despite the closed, sweaty cell of the motel room, a neat man.

In the morning he did a hundred push-ups without stopping for rest. Before he slept, he did the same with sit-ups. He did squats every couple of days. In a way, he did these things as much to combat boredom as to remain fit. His tan faded as the weeks passed.

He was wound tightly and he was fanatically careful. Despite it all, one night while he slept, someone got in and put a six-inch stiletto through his heart.

Rhymer waited outside the open door of the hotel room, shifting uncomfortably from foot to foot as the sun rose higher in the sky, looking like a skinny lizard on a hot rock. Haddox parked his truck, grinding gravel under the tires and kicking up dust.

"Thanks for coming so fast," Rhymer said. He sounded shaky. Haddox saw flecks of something on his collar that looked like oatmeal. Drawing closer to the open door, Haddox smelled the stink of rotting things, of maggot death and spoilage. He wrinkled his nose. His breakfast churned. "God*damn*, Rhymer," he said.

"Yeah, I know. It's something awful, Dan."

There was shade by the door. The inside of the room was a black nothing. Haddox took off his sunglasses and peered inside. He turned back to Rhymer. "You call for a coroner?"

"Right after you."

"And what did they say?"

"Couple of hours. Maybe more."

Haddox considered for a moment. Jefferson Davis County was big and empty, with long roads and stretches of scrub nowhere that took time to cross. They had no coroner's office of their own. For most cases, a local doctor was all anyone needed to produce a death certificate. Tricky situations had to have a real specialist attend, and that meant waiting for someone to come from the next county over.

The stench from inside the room thickened the air between Haddox and his deputy. No one body should reek so badly. He wiped his mouth with the back of his hand, tried not to breathe through his nose. "Who found the body?"

"A Mexican lady that does the rooms."

"And where is she?"

"Up in the office, I think."

"I'm going to go talk to the lady," Haddox said. *Anything to get away from this smell.* "You see to that puddle of puke you left in there, alright?"

"Sure, Dan."

"And when the coroner gets here, make sure you call me 'Sheriff,'" Haddox said. "I don't want them thinking we're a bunch of good ol' boys down here."

"Right, Dan."

Haddox walked away. The hotel was small, just four rooms in a row by the roadside. They were only about a mile from town, but with the quiet they might as well be in the middle of the desert. It was a good place to kill someone.

He passed a rattling air conditioner leaking water onto the cement walk and pushed his way into the office. Like the dead man's hotel room, it was small. The counter was overcrowded with maps and brochures for places far away from here. No one came to Jefferson Davis County for the sights.

When Haddox came in, a man emerged from the back: young and bony-thin. His eyes dropped from Haddox's face to the Sheriff's badge, and then to the holstered Colt. "You Sheriff Haddox?" the man asked.

"I'm him. Who are you?"

"Scott Goodloe. I'm the day manager. I got Mrs. Romulo back here if you want to talk to her."

Haddox put his hands on the counter. He let his gaze wander the narrow space beyond: the stack of truck and gun magazines, the ceramic ashtray with a picture of the Alamo on it and a scratched-up baseball bat with tape wound around the grip. "You ever see that fella lying dead back there?"

"Not when he was dead. I checked him in, though."

"When was that?"

"About six weeks ago. I seen him once or twice going across to the gas station, but that's about it. Seemed like an okay guy."

Haddox looked out the window at the parking lot. "Where's his car?"

"Went a few days ago."

"His car went a few days ago," Haddox said, "and nobody checked that room between now and then?"

"He didn't like anyone to come inside. Look, he was paid for two months, so he *might* have come back. I didn't want him throwing a fit because somebody'd gone into his room."

"He seem like the type to throw a fit about something like that?"

"You'd have to ask Mrs. Romulo."

"I think I will."

The man from the coroner's office turned out to be a sturdy-looking Latino named Zavala. He unloaded two cases of gear from the back of his van, and looked over the hotel room. "How long has this guy been roasting?"

"A few days," Haddox said. "Three, four maybe."

"More like a *week*."

Zavala went in. Haddox lingered on the threshold. Fresh air flowed in from outside, but not enough to make the atmosphere in the room tolerable. Zavala seemed not to notice. He took photographs of the room before turning the lens of his camera on the body. Haddox cast his gaze around, taking note of plastic bags crammed with empty food wrappers, and a collection of empty beer bottles in one corner. He took special note of the Glock semiautomatic on the dresser.

When the photographs were taken, Haddox came in. He stood over the bed. The dead man had been sleeping with his clothes on, his body a gusher of blood surging from the deep wound in his chest. At some point, the killer slashed open the man's pants and cut off his balls. His pallid yellow penis lay in a puddle of coagulated gore.

Zavala put a gloved hand under the corpse, feeling around. He came up with a wallet and then a badge.

"Agent Javier Bainter," the DEA man said. "He was working out of our office in San Miguel de Allende. Been off the reservation for a while now. Close to three months."

"Where's he been?"

"Besides here?" The DEA man scratched his nose. He wore a pinky ring with an enormous diamond set in it. Haddox wondered how any government employee could pull together enough money to afford something like that. "I guess now it doesn't matter."

"You mean you don't care that one of your boys got knifed in my county when he was supposed to be down Mexico way?"

The DEA man shook his head. He smiled a half-smile that didn't last. "Let us worry about the details, Sheriff. The less you know about Bainter, the better."

The phone rang early on a Sunday morning. It took a few rings before Haddox was awake enough to answer. It was Rhymer. "Dan, we just got a call from that hotel again."

Haddox sat up sluggishly. Beers from the night before still lingered in his system. He'd had one for the dead DEA man, Bainter, and then a few more on top of that. He felt headachy and out of sorts. "What's going on?"

"Some Mexican fella came in asking for our dead man. He showed a picture at the front desk, and when they told him what happened, he went hysterical."

"We talking *Mexican* Mexican?"

"Yeah, I think so. The man said 'Mexican.'"

"This Mexican still there?"

"No, he took off."

Haddox forced himself to rise. He wanted to brush his teeth to get the taste out of his mouth. "Listen: you get down there and you find out whatever you can. I want to know what kind of car he was in, if he was alone, everything. You understand? *Everything,* Rhymer."

"Sure thing. Right, Dan."

"I'll be in the truck. You radio me when you know."

Haddox brushed his teeth, washed his face, got dressed and drank coffee. By the time he was on the road, he felt almost like himself. A few minutes later, Rhymer called.

"He was driving a red Cadillac with Mexican plates on it." I got the word out to DPS and the Border Patrol. "Listen, Dan, that picture he showed? He dropped it in the parking lot. I got it here. It's our dead guy, all right. He and the Mexican are all buddy-buddy and drinking margaritas. There's some Spanish writing on the back."

"What's it say?"

"Shit, you know I can't read that."

Haddox banged the steering wheel with the heel of his palm. "All right. Hit the road and see if you can pick up the Mexican's trail."

The radio went quiet. Haddox drove. Maybe this Mexican was the killer, maybe not, but he was real and was more than they had before. Javier Bainter had pictures of his kids in his wallet. Kids needed answers to things like what happened. Every cop knew that.

A half hour later, a DPS officer called over the radio to say he'd found the Mexican and his Cadillac. Haddox put the pedal down. He found the DPS cruiser flashing lights on the side of the road, the Cadillac pulled over and the Mexican in handcuffs.

The photograph said, *Buenos tiempos hoy, mejores tiempos mañana,* which meant, *Good times now, better times tomorrow.* It was dated five months before. Haddox put the picture on the table in front of the Mexican, and then sat down to see what he would do.

Manuel Rodríguez was a young man with a face both pretty and handsome. He had delicate lips. Whenever Haddox looked him in the eye, Rodríguez turned his toward the floor. Haddox didn't think Rodríguez demurred much to anyone; he was packed with lean muscle, especially across the chest and in his shoulders. He resisted the DPS officer when he was pulled over, and he had a livid bruise under his left eye from a baton crack.

Rodríguez looked at the photo without touching it.

Haddox spoke: "¿Quién era él a usted?"

Rodríguez did not answer.

"¿Usted le conocía era muerto?"

Again, nothing.

"I can't do anything for you if I don't understand what's going on," Haddox said.

Rodríguez raised his eyes from the picture, and at the same time he palmed it off the table into his hand. He looked Haddox in the face: "Usted no necesita saber nada."

Haddox opened his mouth to reply. Rhymer knocked on the door of the interview room. The moment passed.

The lawyer's name was Ignacio Pérez. He drove all the way from El Paso to claim Rodríguez. He had a fax machine in his town car, so when he walked through door of the Jefferson Davis County Sheriff's Office, he already had a draft lawsuit in hand. "Not that anything needs to be filed," the lawyer said, "but just in case. Señor Rodríguez shouldn't even be in custody."

Haddox looked over the lawsuit. "No way to be sure about that. Who is Señor Rodríguez, anyway? I'll bet the DEA would like to know."

"If you look, you'll see a letter from the head of the regional DEA supervisor declaring that his agency has no interest in my client. Manuel Rodríguez is not a criminal."

The very last page was a photocopy of a letter on DEA letterhead. Haddox snorted disgustedly and dropped the stack of papers into the trash. He waved a hand toward the closed door of the interview room. "Go ahead, then. I'll sign the paperwork."

Rodríguez's lawyer hustled his client into a waiting Lincoln, and came back to affix his signature to the release papers. Haddox looked out the front window, but could not see Rodríguez in the car; its glass was tinted sheet-black.

"All in a day's work?" Haddox asked the lawyer.

"Señor Rodríguez comes from a respected family, Sheriff Haddox," Pérez replied.

"I'm more concerned about dead cops than respected families."

"Señor Rodríguez had no involvement with Agent Bainter's death."

"I guess I have a problem being so sure about that," Haddox said.

"Well, *I* have no problems lending assistance to help a good man make his way back home." Haddox frowned deeply. Pérez gathered copies of all the forms and stowed them in a slim briefcase. "Are we done, Sheriff?"

"Unless you'd like to have a cup of coffee for the road," Haddox replied sourly.

"No, thank you, Sheriff. Good-bye."

The lawyer left. Haddox watched him through the front windows. The Lincoln drove away, headed west. Haddox waited until the car was completely out of sight before he moved for the door.

"Rhymer, I'm going to take a drive."

"Where you headed, Dan?"

"Just never you mind. And don't try to call me; I'll be off the air."

It took three hours to drive to El Paso. The border was never far from sight. Texas narrowed as it closed on the city, until it was possible to see right over the Rio Grande into Mexico. Just outside the city limits, on the cheap side of the border, stood the Tony Lama boot factory. Tony Lama boots could cost upwards of two hundred dollars a pair in the US, but they were made for pennies on the dollar by Mexican hands.

Haddox kept the Lincoln in sight, though he never drew too close. The town car didn't stop anywhere in the center of city, but at a broad enclosure on the western outskirts of town, surrounded by chain-link fence and paved flat with white concrete that lay blinding in the sun.

Haddox stopped as far back as he could. The enclosure was a truck pen, scattered with panel vans marked with the name and logo of Del Águila Trucking. Pérez parked his car near a bank of diesel pumps and got out. Not far away, a group of men emerged from a converted mobile home turned office.

A pair of binoculars out of the glove compartment gave Haddox a close-up view: Latinos in suits, two of them clearly bodyguards for a third with a mane of white hair and a sharp beard. Rodríguez got out of Pérez's car and stood before the white-haired man, looking at the concrete between their toes. The white-haired man yelled. Rodríguez flinched at the violence of the words. Then the white-haired man slapped Rodríguez hard across the cheek.

Within minutes, the meeting was over. There was more shouting. One of the bodyguard-types gave Pérez an envelope. The white-haired man pointed toward a limousine parked in the shadow of the pre-fab office. Rodríguez went to it meekly. Pérez returned to his Lincoln and drove away. Shortly after, the limousine was on the move. Haddox followed it.

He wasn't sure why he continued to follow, or what he thought he might do. The limousine turned south, and south meant the border and Mexico. Then Haddox's memory flashed on the dead man in the hotel room, stabbed through the heart, his balls sliced off.

He kept going.

Getting *into* Mexico was always easier than getting *out*. On the Texas side, there were maybe a dozen cars waiting to pass through the checkpoint into Mexican territory, while on the far side, traffic stacked up as far as the eye could see. Haddox was two back from the limousine, and when he pulled up to the glass-and-metal booth manned by a Border Patrolman, his police truck drew few glances.

"Howdy, Sheriff," the Border Patrolman said. He glanced down at the Jefferson Davis County seal on the door of the truck. "Kind of a ways out of your bailiwick, aren't you?"

"Just a little," Haddox said. He looked ahead for the limousine. It was caught in a snarl of traffic less than a mile away. They wouldn't slip away from him. "Going across to pick up my mother's arthritis medicine. You know, at the *farmacia*."

They waved Haddox on.

More than anywhere else in Mexico, the band of country that ran along the US/Mexico border was a playground of delights, and every American city had a Mexican mirror. El Paso's was Ciudad Juárez. Buildings were close to each other, businesses stacked one atop the other, the streets crowded with vendors, cars and people. Cheap drugs, legal and illegal, were widely available. Booze and sex, too, for those differently inclined. And for the more timid shopper: T-shirts, straw hats, wooden statues of the Virgin Mary and an endless variety of cut-rate tourist junk.

The limousine drove through this landscape of commerce, until at last it reached a large, cinderblock building painted in fading white. The building was squat and ugly. An enormous picture of a bull was plastered on the wall facing the street, along with chipped, red letters three feet tall: CORRIDA DE TOROS. The name translated literally as *run of bulls*, but it had another meaning: bullfighting.

Haddox parked the truck a block away. Mexicans scattered when they saw the star on the side, even though an Americano badge meant nothing south of the border. Haddox took a weathered leather jacket from underneath the seat and zipped it up tight over his shirt. From a distance, he hoped to look like just another gringo. He kept his gun.

The sky had begun to turn, though evening would not come for a while yet. A cool breeze filtered down to the street from the north. Haddox made his way along a broken sidewalk. The street was a pitted moonscape of potholes and layered in blown dirt. Trash collected against the ragged curb.

He stopped across the street from the bullfighting arena. The place looked about the size of a high-school gymnasium, and badly weathered. This was the kind of place where local enthusiasts could go to see novillos, young bulls for novice bullfighters hoping for a chance to head south to big cities and real arenas, or where the broken-down stars of yesteryear could earn a few pesos from nostalgia.

A few men gathered around the box office, an open window sealed up by a rusty iron grille and shuttered from the inside. A hand-printed bill for the evening was stuck with masking tape to the wall beside the box office. The men spoke animatedly among themselves. More Mexicans gathered, and the volume of their conversation increased. Haddox drew closer.

The corrida enthusiasts parted instinctively when Haddox approached the box office. He knew then that his *copness* was apparent even with his uniform hidden underneath a jacket. The men's talk became muted. One even walked away. Americans were alien at a place like this, and a policeman doubly so.

Haddox examined the bill. There were six bulls, and a list of men involved in the night's battles. Red ink at the top that caught his eye, block letters that declared, ¡CONTRATO ESPECIAL! ¡UNA NOCHE SOLAMENTE! MANUEL GARCÍA RODRÍGUEZ!

"¿Usted tienen gusto del corrida, señor?" asked one of the waiting men. He was older, perhaps in his late fifties. The others looked at Haddox with suspicion, but the old man didn't seem to care. "You like the bullfight?"

Haddox nodded, though it wasn't true. He pointed to Rodríguez's name on the bill. "Do you know this man?"

"Sí. He's from the south. They say he could be the new Manolete. We're lucky to see him. They added him just this morning, you know."

"Manolete," Haddox replied. He looked at the bill again.

At that moment, the rough wooden shutter of the box office opened. A fat woman with a broad mestizo face appeared behind the iron grille. The Mexicans, including the old man, lined up for tickets. They entered the arena through a battered steel door near the corner of the building.

"You want ticket?" the woman asked Haddox. He gave her money and went inside.

The interior of the building smelled like hay, beer and cow shit. Cheap, pull-out bleachers lined three sides of the bullfighting area. The bench seats were gritty with dust. Motes hung in the air, picked out by large electric lights. A pair of men used rakes to smooth out the dun-colored dirt on the killing floor.

Haddox looked around for Rodríguez, the bearded man or even one of the bodyguards. Scratchy, taped music kicked in over the arena loudspeakers. A new odor, that of cooking food, mingled with the rest. During the fight, vendors would sell sweet rolls, beer and other snacks to go with the blood on display.

The bleachers began to fill, almost exclusively with men. The noise level increased. More than once, Haddox heard the name *Manolete* mentioned, often in a raised voice. Almost ninety years later, the Spanish matador who died famously in the ring could still inspire passion.

Haddox explored. He wandered past a makeshift kitchen where a trio of older Mexican women steamed tamales. Haddox's stomach rumbled. He had not eaten all day.

It took ten minutes to find a door that led away from the spectator area and into the workings of the arena. Haddox walked down a narrow hallway into an invisible barrier of bull-smell that grew stronger and stronger with every step. He turned a corner and stopped; one of the bodyguards from the limousine stood at attention outside a plain, closed door.

Haddox knew it would be easy to turn away now. The doubt that danced at the corner of his mind all day, first as he trailed Pérez and then as he followed the limousine beyond the border of Texas into Ciudad Juárez, returned. He chased it away with the same prod: Javier Bainter.

The bodyguard saw Haddox. He crossed his arms across his chest to make himself seem bigger. Haddox was six-three. As he came closer, he figured the bodyguard as an inch or two taller.

"Hola, amigo," Haddox said. "Quiero hablar con Rodríguez."

"Consiga perdido," the bodyguard replied.

"I just want to talk to him."

"¡Dije consigo perdido!"

The bodyguard put out a hand to push Haddox away. Haddox grabbed the Mexican by the wrist and turned, twisting with the movement until suddenly he was behind the bigger man with a firm armlock in place. The bodyguard pushed with his legs. Haddox rode with it. He steered the Mexican headfirst into the wall. Skull and concrete made a hollow sound together. The bodyguard crumpled.

Haddox looked up and down the hall. No one was around. The sound of feet on the wooden bleachers in the arena and the rising noise of chatter carried through the walls. He tried the door and found it unlocked.

Rodríguez was there. He turned away from a mirror ringed with bright lightbulbs, one hand still holding the brush he used to apply his dark eyeliner. His expression was surprised, but not shocked. For an instant, it almost seemed as if Rodríguez had expected him, just not at that moment.

The young man was half-dressed in his traje de luces, the "suit of lights" that was instantly recognizable anywhere in the world as the garb of the bullfighter. Rodríguez had not yet donned his jacket, and he sat naked below the waist on a folding metal chair. The pants he would wear, the teleguillas, took two men to put on. Perhaps the bodyguard was to help.

Rodríguez's gaze passed beyond Haddox to the hallway and the sprawled form of the unconscious bodyguard. "Close the door, please."

Haddox did as he was asked. The dressing room was tiny and cramped. There was not even a shower, only a deep sink that looked like something a janitor would use to fill buckets. "You're speaking English now," he said.

Rodríguez turned back to the mirror. He applied his eyeliner with an air of practice. "I speak good English."

"Did you practice with Javier Bainter?"

Rodríguez turned his attention to his hair. He applied pomade and sculpted his dark locks into perfection with a comb. He was handsome and quietly calm, with no trace of the sorrow he showed in the Jefferson Davis County jailhouse. When he tried on his montera, the twin-pointed hat of the matador, he looked at his reflection in open appraisal. "You should not have come here."

"I had to know. Who was he to you? What did you want with him?"

Rodríguez removed the hat. He watched Haddox in the mirror. "In the corrida de toros, the matador is all. The other fighters come and go, but the matador commands the respect of everyone who watches him. He is wanted by women and envied by men. That is me."

"You don't fight in places like this. You fight in the south, in real arenas."

"I fight wherever I am told to fight. I go when I am ordered to go."

"Who was the man who brought you here?"

"My father. He wants me to fight tonight. Any fight will do. And if I perform as he commands, then everything will be forgotten. My leaving, my disobedience… everything I have done."

Rodríguez touched the corner of his eye. Whether it was to make a tiny adjustment to his makeup, or to dispatch a tear, Haddox didn't know. But abruptly he knew something else: "You were Bainter's lover."

"I am a lover of women," Rodríguez said without energy.

"Who killed Javier Bainter?" Haddox asked.

In the mirror, Rodríguez looked Haddox in the eyes. "I don't know. I will never know. That is how my father insists it must be."

"I can't—" Haddox began.

"You *can*. You must. There is nothing else."

Haddox exhaled sharply and leaned against the wall of the cramped dressing room. Rodríguez rose from his seat, and Haddox saw the man's penis dangling between thighs of lean muscle. "This can't be all," Haddox said.

"The matador is a man," Rodríguez said. "*Completely* a man. And it was the same for Javier. We could not be anything else, even though we wanted to."

Rodríguez kept his back to Haddox and donned his cha-quetilla, the bright and beautiful jacket of the suit of lights. Haddox tried to imagine Rodríguez and the dead man together, but it was impossible... impossible in more than one way. His head spun. He felt smothered in this undersized room.

"Have you heard that they call me the next Manolete?" Rodríguez asked without turning around.

"I heard that."

"Manolete was gored to death, you know. And the bull was afeitado. You know what this means? He had his horns shaved to protect the matador. Manolete should have been safe. He should have walked from the plaza de toros without a drop of his blood shed." Rodríguez looked over his shoulder. "Even the best matador can be beaten by a clever bull. It is a good way to die."

Haddox opened the door of the dressing room. His hand shook. Rodríguez did not watch him go. Haddox retreated down the hallway, his thoughts whirling, until he emerged beneath the bleachers into the roar of a bullfight already underway. He headed for the exit, and then out into the gathering night.

He felt sick to his stomach, the smells of the arena curdling at the back of his throat. He looked down the street. A familiar figure was there: the white-bearded man. The second bodyguard moved with his master, and both paused when they saw Haddox. For a long moment, Haddox and the old man watched each other, and then the elder Rodríguez disappeared inside.

It took only a couple of minutes to return to his truck. He got behind the wheel and started the engine, but he didn't drive away. Instead, he watched the ugly lump of the bullfighting arena, vaguely conscious of the engine's vibration through the steering wheel, thinking only of the young matador called Manuel Rodríguez, and the dead man he loved.

An hour later, an ambulance arrived. Corrida fans spilled out into the street in turmoil. Medics beat their way through the press of bodies, handling a folded stretcher like a battering ram. When they emerged, Haddox couldn't see who they carried, but he knew. He wondered if Rodríguez would live long enough to reach a hospital.

He waited until the ambulancia tore away with a screech of rubber, leaving behind the crowd of wailing fans. Then he waited a few minutes more, until even its siren had vanished. When enough time had passed, Haddox put the truck in gear and drove away.

He wanted to be out of Mexico, and he never wanted to come back.

AFTERWORD

WHERE GOD AND THE DEVIL
WHEEL LIKE VULTURES
By
TOM RUSSELL
(September 2009)

There's a story here, but it exists in illogical fragments, chaotic subtexts, and poverty economics cured in the meth-soaked algebra of need, greed and corruption. And eventually it all plays out in song. Folk songs, cowboy ballads and narcocorridos. What you can't see with your eyes you can feel in your heart. Hand me down my old guitar. —TR

Down below El Paso lies Juarez. Mexico is different, *like the travel poster says...*

—Burt Bacharach
& Bob Hilliard
"Mexican Divorce"

I. Touch of Evil

That was the summer of "birds falling out of trees," as the Apaches might say. Looming weirdness. I'm in a beat-up Juarez taxi cab, inching slowly away from the Plaza Monumental bullring. A masked character in the truck across from us begins firing an automatic weapon over the top of the cab. Across the street at the Geronimo bar, three bodies fall into the gutter. My cab driver pulls his head down and shrieks: *Cristo! Cristo!* against the racket of trumpets and accordions from a narcocorrido song on the radio. *Cristo, Jesu Cristo! Ayuda me!* The cab lurches forward with each string of Jesus curses. I'm riding inside a pinball machine set up next to a shooting gallery. Bodies are falling outside. Bodies are falling in the drug song on the radio. My shirtsleeve is stuck on the handle of the door and I can't seem to twist and duck my head down below the dashboard. *This is not the way I want to die.* I try to grab hold of the wheel but the driver pulls himself together, makes the sign of the cross, then turns down back streets and alleys that lead to the border bridge. The rat-a-tat-tat of a weapon fades into the distance. The cabbie wheels to a stop and lights a cigarette. *Sangre de Cristo. Fifty pesos, por favor.*

It's another Sunday evening in Ciudad Juarez.

Back then, twelve years ago, it cost fifteen cents to enter Mexico. Fifteen cents to wheel through the turnstile and cross the river bridge into the carnal trap. *The Lawless Roads.* I used to think of Orson Welles' noir classic *Touch of Evil* when I walked down the bridge into Ciudad Juarez. That sinister feeling which draws the gringo-rube into web of rat-ass bars and neon caves; the nerve tingling possibility of cheap drink, violence, and sex; sex steeped in sham clichés about dark-eyed senoritas and donkey shows. It's that heady, raw — *anything goes, all is permitted, death is to be scorned* — routine which informed and carved out the rank borderline personalities of John Wesley Hardin, Billy the Kid, Pancho Villa and hundreds of Mexican drug lords. Western myth, now grim reality. You craved the real west, didn't you?

The late British writer, Graham Greene, knew the border terrain. He crossed over at Laredo in 1939, noting: "The border means more than a custom's house, a passport office, a man with a gun. Over there everything is going to be different. Life is never going to be quite the same again after your passport is stamped and you find yourself speechless among the money changers."

Speechless among the money changers. I like that. I can't imagine what Hunter Thompson would have come up with if he'd written a version of *Fear and Loathing* about the current state of affairs in Juarez. *Cristo, Cristo, Cristo.* Thompson once said that if you want to know where the edge is, you've got to *go over* it. Juarez is big time over the edge.

The next Sunday, following my shooting gallery ride, I decide I'll visit Juarez again. Pushing my luck. I was *in between relationships* that season, and in a reckless mood. Perhaps I bought all that *laughing at death* routine in the lyrics of tequila drenched Charro songs. I crossed over the Santa Fe bridge and caught a bus toward the bull plaza, then wandered into the Geronimo bar, drained a Tecate, and left. I walked back toward the bridge. I was a quarter mile away when shots rang down the crowded avenue near the Geronimo. Two more bodies fell into the gutter. *Cristo!*

It was 1997. These were incipient skirmishes in a violent plague they now call a full-on "drug war." The twelve-year war is currently overheating; the Mexican army patrols the river with jeeps pulling canon-sized machine guns, and the body counts are higher than Baghdad. The old border town ain't the same. The bullring has been torn down to make a Wal-Mart; the tourist market is empty, and the Mariachi's have all gone south. Whorehouse madams are cooking up batches of crystal meth aimed for farm kids in Kansas, Iowa and Nebraska. Everything's gone straight to hell, since Sinatra played Juarez.

A week ago the headlines of the Spanish language paper read: *Daylight shootouts, Burned Bodies, and Dead Children.* Yesterday the offering was: A *Thunder of fourty three Corpses in the Morgue in seventy two Hours.* Meanwhile the English speaking paper, on the El Paso side of the river, featured a headline about someone resigning from our local school board. A little denial goes a long way here on the sunny side. It's tradition. Graham Greene, again, in 1939: "…no day passed (in Mexico) without somebody's being assassinated somewhere; at the end of the paper there was a page for tourists. That page never included the shootings, and the tourists, as far as I could see, never read the Spanish pages. They lived in a different world….with *Life* and *Time*…they were impervious to Mexico."

In El Paso, the refutation melts into absurdity. This morning's El Paso paper announced that the "John Wesley Hardin Secret Society" would meet at six p.m. in the Concordia cemetery. There would be "old west re-enactors and six gun shoot-outs" commemorating the night Hardin met his demise on the streets of old El Paso. Hardin was an outlaw who claimed he'd killed forty-two people before he went to prison in 1878. When he was released, brandishing a law degree, Hardin moved to El Paso and went back to his old ways. One night Sheriff John Selman shot him in the back of the head, then drug the body out into the El Paso street so the locals could gawk at another dead lawyer with a big mouth.

Five years ago the City Council was entertaining the idea of a giant Old West theme park in downtown El Paso. Something to lure the tourists from Germany and Japan. Shooting re-enactments and dance hall girls; three shows a day. But what the hell do we need that for? We have Juarez a quarter mile away and it costs a few pennies to cross over. Or tourists could set up chairs on top the Holiday Inn Express and bring their binoculars.

This morning, after the John Wesley Hardin story, I turned that page in section B where there was a short item about two El Pasoans slain yesterday in a Juarez bar shooting. Back page stuff. Hidden near the end of the story was the astounding body count: *nearly two thousand nine hundred people, including more than one hundred and sixty this month alone, have been killed in Juarez since a war between drug traffickers erupted January 2008.* John Wesley Hardin wouldn't stand a chance.

Two thousand nine hundred bodies in twenty months. Welcome to the frontier, where "God and the Devil wheel like vultures, and a loose fences separates the good man from the bad." *(Nicholas Shakespeare on Graham Greene.)* We are walking the streets between doubt and clarity; savage reality and indifference. Shooting re-enactments and World War Three. This is El Paso-Juarez, an extreme western edge of Texas that no

Texan east of Sierra Blanca would lay claim to. The wild, non-fictional Mexican West. Hollywood and a million dime novels never quite got it right. Sam Peckinpah wasn't even close. El Paso-Juarez is the American frontier in every sense: *the land or territory which forms the furthest extent of a country's settled or inhabited regions. The outer limit. (Webster's Unabridged.)*

And now, September 4, 2009, as I was trying to put this essay to rest, the biggest shoot-out in the history of Juarez took place in a Juarez drug clinic. Seventeen people slaughtered. The carnage hit the front page of the *New York Times* and, even weirder, the front page of the El Paso Times: *Juarez in Shock: Attack Considered City's Worst Multiple Shooting.* The New York Times coverage sounded as if it were lifted from a James Ellroy novel: *"a thick layer of blood covered the concrete floor...a chained dog had been shot...the smell of death hung in the air."* God and the Devil, wheeling like vultures.

And finally, it's September 11, 2009, and while the world is remembering 9/11 and the twin towers going down, there's a little item on page 9A of the *El Paso Times*: "It is not uncommon for U.S. citizens to be part of Mexican drug cartels because cartels have placed cells in more than two hundred cities across the United States. According to the Department of Justice, Mexican cartels...pose the greatest organized-crime threat to the United States and its people."

Incomprehensible? You have to understand the full contextual layout: cultural, geographic, historical. Then dim the lights and listen to the music: either Dylan's "Just like Tom Thumb's Blues," or Marty Robbin's "El Paso," or one of a thousand narcocorrido songs where the bad guy is the good guy, and behind every lyrical gravestone is buried a lost verse to "The Streets of Laredo." This is gunfighter country.

II. The Place of Dead Roads / Mean as Hell

"The fact is, Old Boy, the land is so poor
I don't think you could use it as a hell anymore/
But to sweeten the deal and get it off my hands
I'll water this place with the Rio Grande..."

— God Talking to the Devil, Johnny Cash,
"Mean as Hell"

When Horace Greely said "Go West Young Man," he could not have been aiming the kid in the direction of El Paso-Juarez. Naw. Not unless he had a twisted sense of humor, or the young man he was chatting with was Billy *the* Kid, who was born in the Bronx. But off I went.

In 1997 I moved to El Paso, traveling two thousand four hundred miles in a U-Haul Truck and across the width of Texas. From the blues-drenched East Texas thickets and on through the boggy midlands and rusty oil derricks of the dying swap meet towns. On out toward the Chihuahuan desert. You don't know Texas unless you driven the width. Four hundred miles west of Austin the air begins to dry out, the birds of prey grow larger, and the land flattens out into a reddish-orange sand punctuated with dwarf Mesquites and Palo Verdes. The surface of the earth looks like Mexican flan that's been left in the oven too long. You've got a few hundred miles to go. Carry water.

As you hit the city limits, if it's night, you'll see a carpet of the ten million blinking lights over in Ciudad Juarez. El Paso is the sleepy 1950s old west town laid out on the front of that carpet. To the left is the vintage Plaza Hotel — one of the first Hiltons; on the top floor is the penthouse where Liz Taylor lived with Nicky Hilton. The Plaza's been closed for years. Hell, the town has been semi-dead for pretty much half a century. If you turn off towards downtown you'll hit the central plaza with its fountain and the fiberglass sculptures of leaping alligators. Up until the 1960s there were real gators in there, but too many drunks fell in and lost essential limbs. Local color abounds.

Most people don't exit Interstate 10. They sail through this sleepy downtown and avert their eyes from the poverty shacks of Juarez; keep right on going towards Tucson or Los Angeles. The Promised Land lies elsewhere. Interstate 10 finally dead-ends into the Santa Monica pier, near the antique merry-go-round where you can whirl your kids around in the Pacific sea air, knowing you made it through hell and the badlands.

Occasionally a tourist from Frankfurt or Des Moines will make the unwise decision of turning off; driving the kids over the bridge into Juarez in search of "a real taco." That might be a very bad mistake, senor. The rules are different on the other side.

Johnny Cash once recorded a recitation titled "Mean as Hell," in which The Devil is looking for a hell on earth, and God gives him a plot near the Rio Grande which sounds like El Paso. That might have been after Cash was busted here for smuggling ten thousand pills over from Juarez. Ah, the history! Wasn't it Raymond Chandler who quipped: "No one cared if I died or moved to El Paso?" That quote was ringing in my ears as I stopped here and unloaded the truck. I was home. It was a long long way from Brooklyn. Fourteen miles and half a century. In El Paso there was no music scene, no resort hotels, and no welcome wagon. Suited me. So many critics had called me an "outsider" I finally decided to go find where the American outside really *was*.

I bought a 1930s historic adobe on three acres and settled down to hide and write songs and novels. I was surrounded by rock walls, barbed wire and cactus. Cormac McCarthy lived in a rattle trap adobe up on the mountain; trying to do the same thing. *To be left alone to write.* Unfortunately fame and fans hunted Cormac down and chased him away to Santa Fe. I'm still here. St. Thomas of the Desert in this dry wasteland where extremes meet. Where men balance their own aridity and desire for reclusiveness with that of the landscape. Like the desert fathers in Egypt, I came here not to find my identity so much as to lose it, eradicate an old personality and reinvent a new one. *Society is a cave; the way out is solitude.* But there's a deep history here which begins to claw at you. The history seeps into your spirit and begins to inform the writing with that odd and tangled chaotic soul of the borderlands.

Five hundred years ago a Spaniard, Don Juan de Onate, rode his tall Andalusian horse across the river and claimed this land for Spain. The boys sat down and rested on the riverbank and roasted up a few javelinas. It was the first Thanksgiving in America, years ahead of that Plymouth Rock routine. A few hundred years later Pancho Villa rode up and down this same river terrorizing the citizenry; changing his political allegiances as often as he changed his favorite ice cream flavors; marrying dozens of women at a time for the cause of the Revolution. Villa inspired a thousand folk songs and corridos; countless books and movies. His mythical shadow is long. Ask any soldier in a drug cartel.

Later Villa attacked Columbus, New Mexico, and the U.S. sent Black Jack Pershing, with young George Patton in tow, but they never caught him. There's not much about that in our grammar school history books. America had been attacked and invaded and we couldn't catch the rotten bandito, even though he was only a few hundred miles away. Sound familiar? We could not follow the signs or the spoors; and the blood spoors on this desert can be traced back hundreds of years, beyond Mexico and Christian Spain, to the Moors. Those bastards, the Moors! They sat a horse pretty damn good. They were the forefathers of the modern American cowboy and they rode their little Arab ponies hell-bent on bloodlust. And you couldn't catch 'em.

During the Mexican revolution the people along the American side of the Rio Grande would take chairs up on their roofs and watch the war on the other side through field glasses. The late El Paso painter, Tom Lea, shared that anecdote with me. He died a few years ago; he taught me many things about this "wonderful country," including the fact that Pancho Villa had put a price on young Tom's head when he was six years old. Tom's father was the Sheriff of El Paso and kicked Villa back across the river a few times. *Get the hell out of here you saddle-faced son of a bitch.* Little Tom had to have a bodyguard to go to school. Things ain't changed a hell of a lot. There's an outlaw feel in each little cloud hanging over my potted agaves.

I crossed the Santa Fe bridge many times in 1997 and heard the rat-a-tat-tat which foreshadowed the rumor of a coming war. After those initial skirmishes came a plague of murdered women. A modern horror story. Hundreds of female bodies dug up in the desert surrounding Juarez. Serial murders? Drug war casualties? Maquiladora workers who walked home late at night? The rash of killings has never been fully explained. Hillary Clinton, in addressing human rights violations and rape in the African Congo, talked about women being the first victims on the front lines of wars against humanity. Holds true in Juarez. A few years ago, Hollywood and dozens of journalists came; books were written. Movies were released. Hollywood went home. Committed actresses turned their attentions to other "third world" causes. Or began adopting babies in Somalia. In Juarez matters got worse. A huge black cross went up on the Juarez side of the bridge with hundreds of railroad spikes hammered into it. One for every murdered woman. The sign at the top said: *"ni una mas."* *Not one more.*

But the carnage spread out, disregarding gender and age. The full war was on. The media forgot about the dead women. The headlines, if there were any, were about the "war against drugs," listing facts baked in the tired rhetoric of presidents and army generals. This time the victims were women, men and babies. You can't be too precise with an automatic weapon. Not if you're wired to the gills on crack and sotol. Not if you're firing in a crowded bar or bus station. So the Mexican president called in the army.

III. It Isn't Going Away and Nobody is Going to Destroy It

When I walked out into my cactus garden this morning, I heard that familiar old rat-a-tat-tat of automatic gunfire drifting through the Cottonwood trees to the south. Or was that a cadre of nail guns from the mushrooming housing developments which have ruined the last of our upper Rio Grande farming Valley? You never know. The cartels would be stupid to carry the war over to this side, but the corruption on both sides of the river is pervasive and deep. It effects most of the almost three million people who try to live in this valley the Spaniards called El Paseo del Norte.

El Paso is an abandoned midway of cultural impoverishment. I've always wondered why we didn't have the amenities of San Antonio or, say, Tucson or Phoenix. There are no resorts, tourist attractions, or Whole Foods stores, and even precious few decent restaurants with an outdoor patio. Years ago the city planners could have diverted part of the river into downtown and capitalized on the scenery, in the tradition of as San Antonio. El Paso might have rivaled Tucson as a desert destination; a retirement haven. The climate is a little more temperate than Tucson or Phoenix. But when corporations and big business came calling, decades ago, the city council and powers-that-be delivered the ultimatum, which went something like: *We'll allow you to move in here, but what are you going to do for us?* Big Money squirmed with distaste and waltzed away.

Downtown El Paso looks much the same as 1955, except the historic storefronts are now bargain Korean "fashion" joints, Mexican CD outlets, and pawn shops. Oh, there's a new art museum, the Camino Real hotel, and a renovated theater; but the rest of downtown seems an extension or Juarez. Instead of revitalizing the downtown, the city council allowed a handful of housing developers to go out and destroy the upper and lower irrigated farming valleys along the Rio Grande. Thousands of acres of prime agricultural land were traded off for a quick shot, hangdog economy based around cheap houses which will collapse in thirty years; long before a few hundred thousand Mexican families have paid off their long-term mortgages. And there you have it. The seven capital sins dance like harpies along this riverbank: Pride, covetousness, lust, anger...and the Queen Bee Mother, *corruption. What are you going to do for us? Cristo!*

But you're interest in the body count, no? *The drug war.* And the bottom line or the big *Why* of it all? Amigo, the real story will not be delivered by presidents, politicians, army generals, police sergeants, newscasters, DEA agents, sociologists, dead-line journalists, and all those whose livelihoods dance around the twisting of that murky little gap between doubt and clarity. Fact and furor. Pride and paranoia. The slant and the spin. In the kingdoms of the blind and corrupt, the one-eyed billionaire drug lord is King. Always and forever.

Tucson author Charles Bowden is able to give you the lowdown; he may be our most capable and truthful witness. Bowden surmises that it's "nonsense" that the United States and Mexican governments are partners in a war *against* drugs. He calls it a war *for* drugs as the Mexican economy collapses. Here's Bowden on the employment of the Mexican Army:

"They've moved into Ciudad Juarez and the murder rate has exploded there. There's eight thousand to ten thousand federal troops and Federal police now in Juarez. In 2007, there were three hundred murders, a record for the city. But is 2008, there were one thousand six hundred people slaughtered. This year there's been over one thousand two hundred people slaughtered. That's the achievement of the Mexican army. Every place they go they've terrified people…the soldiers run amok." (democracynow.org 8/11/09)

Bowden asserts that Mexico would sink without drug money because the oil fields are collapsing down there, and Mexico earns up to fifty billion dollars a year in foreign currency from selling drugs. Bowden's summation: "Drugs have penetrated the whole culture, and it isn't going away. And nobody is going to destroy it."

And the guns over there? Most of them come from the United States. It's estimated that over two thousand a day cross the border into Mexico. There's only one gun store in Mexico, in Mexico City, and you have to be a cop or a government official or an army person to get in there. The drugs come back across the other way. Marijuana, cocaine, heroin, and the newest and most deadly frontrunner: crystal meth. As the United States cleans up our own meth labs and regulates pseudo ephedrine in cold tablets (needed to make meth), Mexican cartels have risen to the occasion; a purer form is now being manufactured over there. Most of it comes back across this river.

And what do we do with these gruesome facts? Hell, we juggle them up and down and pretend we're appalled; slide them across the news monitors; then jam them into folders, reports and journals no one reads. This is old territory for me. My master's degree was in criminology. Then I became a songwriter, and part of that transition was sparked by the frustration was dealing with a *Social Science* which operates on the wasteful billion dollar dole of research grants, and then publishes findings and statistics in a sterile academic vacuum. Journals hidden in dusty library stacks. I told my old criminology mentor, back in 1969, that the world would be better off if he published his findings in *Playboy*, or the *New Yorker*, or even *The Reader's Digest*, rather than these dry and sterile journals which preached to the academic choir. Then I picked up my guitar and waltzed away. Bob Dylan was more of an agent for social change than C. Wright Mills.

So what's the *good news*, Tom? Why the hell would anyone stay in El Paso?

IV. Last Stand in Patagonia

Everything in nature is lyrical in its ideal essence; tragic in its fate, and comic in its existence.

—George Santayana

El Paso is my own Patagonia. Outside and over the edge. Lyrical in its essence, tragic in its fate; comic in its existence. But, it's a peaceful place. You find that amusing? The war has not spilled across the Rio Bravo. Life is simple and cheap. I like the people. There are ten thousand Mexican restaurants, and the sun going down on the Franklin Mountains always elicits my daily prayer of gratitude. Life seems more precious on the last, wild frontier. There is a raw beauty and a lack of pretense. And that wonderful history which has seeped into my blood; emptying into song and story.

I irrigate my fruit trees from the Rio Grande and think of the days when Sinatra and Nat King Cole and the Kingston Trio played down river in Juarez. The days of the "quickie divorce" Burt Bacharach wrote about. Marilyn Monroe divorced Arthur Miller in Juarez, then strolled down to the Kentucky Club and bought the house a round of Margaritas. Hell, the Margarita was *invented* in Juarez in the late 1940s. Gypsy Rose Lee stripped at The Palace Club and Manolete fought in the bullring. Steve McQueen died over there in a clinic. This is a place to write and to absorb the history. A place to be left alone to create and conjure up your own meaning to events on either side of the river. Forget about the final answers. They will not be forthcoming.

Our gun laws are not going to change. Certain drugs will not be legalized. The drug cartels will never disappear. These are people supporting what's left of the Mexican economy. Some drug czars are revered in narco-songs and others might throw monetary support the local village schools and hospitals. The "war" will either be fought to a conclusion or go underground, like a hidden desert river which appears hundreds of miles away. Always running with human blood. *Cristo. Jesus Cristo.*

I'll watch it all go down from Ardovino's Desert Crossing, the great bar and restaurant which sits up near Mt. Cristo Rey, overlooking the lights of El Paso. (*Okay, there are a few good bars here.*) Trains roll cross the mountain at happy hour and border patrol trucks chase illegals through these desperate, yucca-choked rocks and rills. Over yonder the ugly black border wall snakes across the sandy hills. The wall is our knee-jerk attempt to intimidate Mexican illegals who want to do the dirty work we shun. But this is still the Old West, amigo. Those class equations have always been such. The Chinese built the railroads with a shotgun at their head, and their opium was always available in the back of the chop suey joints and whorehouses. The "greasers" and "chinks" did the dirty work; and those red devil Apaches raided our horse camps until we sent Geronimo down to Florida to chill out. We're getting it under control, ain't we? It's the coked-up, Manifest Destiny politics of Methland.

These are the far regions and outer limits of America. *La Frontera*. We've twisted and exploited and mined the Old West for those clichéd, watered-down versions of violent cowboy and Indian stories, where John Wayne kicks ass and rides away in a white hat. Now it's the drug soldiers and assassins in baseball caps who hold court with submachine guns, which we sold 'em. *They're* the ones kicking ass. You can write it from any political angle and subtext. You can walk around leaning on the moral, self-righteous crutch of whatever religion and political party or news magazines you subscribe to. The palaver don't cut much on the backstreets of Juarez. There's a story here, but it exists in illogical fragments, chaotic subtexts, and poverty economics cured in the meth-soaked algebra of need, greed and corruption. And eventually it all plays out in song. Folk songs, cowboy ballads and narcocorridos. What you can't see with your eyes you can feel in your heart. Hand me down my old guitar.

But hell, it's sundown. I'm parched. The mountains are turning crimson and the beer is cold. The rat-a-tat-tat might be gunfire, or the ice in the blender over there in the Mecca bar. I'll leave you to your safe and well-edited taste of doom flashing across the six o'clock news. Somebody inside the bar has played Dylan's "Just Like Tom Thumb's Blues," and for a brief moment I have all the poetic details I need about the frontier and these borderlands I've come to love. But no answers, amigo. Never any real answers. Only a noir lyricism which drifts out between the comic and the tragic.

> *"When you're lost in the rain in Juarez*
> *And it's Easter time too*
> *And your gravity fails and negativity*
> *Don't pull you through*
> *Don't put on any airs*
> *when you're down*
> *on Rue Morgue avenue...."*
> —Bob Dylan

Tom Russell, El Paso-Juarez, September 11, 2009

NOW

A young man and his pregnant wife, sitting in the lowest-rung cantina in Tubutama.

The coyote looks them both over. The young man can't be much more than twenty. He earlier said that he was originally from Sonora. He wears raggedy Levis, worn boots and a too-small T-shirt promoting the film *Once Upon A Time in Mexico*.

The coyote figures if these two ever reach the other side, the kid will spend at least the next five years of his life working for chump change hanging drywall for new, shittily constructed gringo houses.

And the young woman—hardly more than a girl, really? The coyote figures her for eighteen, or less. She is already running to pudgy, the unwanted pregnancy like some spur to her waiting fat cells.

Mexican women rarely lose their baby weight. Well, hardly any of them living in Mexico seemed to.

The girl has dyed her hair some J-Lo bogus shade of honey brown—some hue no Latina was ever born with. But the girl is smart enough to know she shouldn't color her hair while carrying a kid: her roots are growing in black. There is a black stripe about three inches wide at her part. The coyote guesses her for five, maybe six months pregnant.

She stands and excuses herself. Her man—husband? boyfriend?—waits until she is gone and says, "With the baby, she drinks anything, well, you know, her kidneys…"

"I have many sisters," the coyote says. He smiles, revealing gold front teeth. "They get big with child, it's constant pissing, I know, brother."

"I'm not sure we should even be thinking about this," the young man says. "I mean, with her like this now. Maybe it is better if we wait."

The coyote waves a hand. "Be *harder* then. Then you have *three* bellies to carry water for." The coyote is overdue on a payment for his new Hummer. He needs the money, so he says, "No, you go *now*. Now, every drink she takes, it's a drink the nino gets, sí? And you're young, strong. You'll carry your woman, it comes to that, yes?"

"Well, sure, but—"

"A baby, out there, crossing in August? Early September? Even October? You'd lose the child. Better to go now, while she still is a few months out and when you both have two arms to carry the water. When you're not weighed down with a baby. You go *now*. Before the Minute Men increase their numbers. Before fucking Bush puts more National Guard on the border. Before they build more of that goddamn wall."

"You take many across," the young man says, almost decided, "where do they all go?"

The coyote smiles again, flashing his gold teeth. He says, "I hear very good things about a place called O-hi-o."

CONTRIBUTORS

Ken Bruen is one of the most prominent Irish crime writers of the last two decades. Born in Galway, he spent twenty-five years traveling the world before he began writing in the mid 1990s. As an English teacher, Bruen worked in South Africa, Japan, and South America, where he once spent a short time in a Brazilian jail. The Edgar® finalist also has two long-running series: one starring a disgraced former policeman named Jack Taylor, the other a London police detective named Inspector Brant. Praised for their sharp insight into the darker side of today's prosperous Ireland, Bruen's novels are marked by grim atmosphere and clipped prose. Among the best known are his *White Trilogy* (1998-2000) and *The Guards* (2001), the Shamus award-winning first novel in the Jack Taylor series.

Jim Cornelius grew up in Southern California. Not the SoCal of swimming pools and movie stars — the SoCal of rugged mountains and Joshua Tree-studded deserts. He broke out to make his living with his pen in shadow of the Cascade Mountains in Central Oregon, where he runs the woods, plays music with The Anvil Blasters and tells true stories of hard men in dangerous territory. He is the author of the forthcoming

Warriors of the Wild Lands: True Tales of the Frontier Partisans and the keeper of the blog FrontierPartisans.com.

Garnett Elliott lives and works in Tucson, though he grew up in the mean old border town of Yuma, Arizona. Previous stories have appeared in *Alfred Hitchcock's Mystery Magazine, Thuglit, Needle: A Magazine of Noir*, and numerous online publications. He is also a contributing author to the acclaimed Drifter Detective series put out by Beat to a Pulp Books. You can follow him on Twitter @TonyAmtrak.

Bradley Mason Hamlin is an American writer and the creator of the Intoxicated Detective series. He is an alumni of the University of California, where poet Gary Snyder dubbed Hamlin "The Road Warrior of Poetry!" Born in Los Angeles, Hamlin currently lives in Sacramento, California with his wife, Nicky Christine, and their children & their wild cats. His latest book of poems, *California Blonde*, is available from Black Shark Press. For more information, please see: http://mysteryisland.net

Sam Hawken is the Crime Writers Association Dagger-nominated author of *The Dead Women of Juárez, Tequila Sunset, Missing* and *La Frontera*. He makes his home in Maryland with his wife and son.

Mike MacLean is best known for writing the hit Syfy movies *Sharktopus, Piranhaconda*, and *Dinocroc vs. Supergator*, all produced by the legendary Roger Corman. Before his foray into creature features, Mike wrote hardboiled fiction that appeared in *The Best American Mystery Stories* (Alongside his literary idols Elmore Leonard and James Lee Burke), *Ellery Queen's Mystery Magazine*, and *Thuglit*. Recently, Mike has embarked on a career in comic books, collaborating on *Lady Death* with her creator Brian Pulido. You can nerd out with Mike online at mikemaclean.net.

Craig McDonald is an award-winning author and journalist. The Hector Lassiter series has been published to international acclaim in numerous languages. *Head Games*, McDonald's debut novel, was nominated for Edgar®, Anthony and Gumshoe awards in the U.S. and the 2011 Sélection du prix polar Saint-Maur en Poche in France. His novel about illegal immigration's impact on a small Ohio town, *El Gavilan*, earned a starred review from *Publishers Weekly* in 2011. You can find him on the web at craigmcdonaldbooks.com.

Manuel Ramos is a retired lawyer and the author of eight published novels and one short story collection. For his professional and community service he has received the Colorado Bar Association's Jacob V. Schaetzel Award, the Colorado Hispanic Bar Association's Chris Miranda Award, the Spirit of Tlatelolco Award, and others. His fiction has garnered the Colorado Book Award, the Chicano/Latino Literary Award, the Top Hand Award from the Colorado Authors League, and three Honorable Mentions from the Latino International Book Awards. His first novel, *The Ballad of Rocky Ruiz*, was a finalist for the Edgar® award from the Mystery Writers of America and won the Colorado Book Award in the Fiction category. His published works include *Desperado: A Mile High Noir*, winner of the 2014 Colorado Book Award in the Mystery category, several short stories, poems, non-fiction articles and a handbook on Colorado landlord-tenant law, now in a sixth edition. He is a co-founder of and regular contributor to La Bloga (www.labloga.blogspot.com), an award-winning Internet magazine devoted to Latino literature, culture, news, and opinion. *The Skull of Pancho Villa and Other Stories* was published in 2015.

Stephen D. Rogers is the author of *Shot to Death* and more than nine hundred shorter works. His website, www.StephenDRogers.com, includes a list of new and upcoming titles as well as other timely information.

Tom Russell's songs have been recorded by such icons as Johnny Cash, Dave Van Ronk, Jerry Jeff Walker, Doug Sahm, Joe Ely, Nanci Griffith, Iris Dement, and Ramblin' Jack Elliott, among others. Lawrence Ferlinghetti, the legendary poet, has said that he shares "a great affinity with Tom Russell's songs, for he is writing out of the wounded heart of America." His songs have appeared in a dozen movies and television series including *The Road to Nowhere, Tremors, Songcatcher* and *Northern Exposure*. He has published a detective novel (in Scandinavia), a compendium of songwriting quotes, *And Then I Wrote*, and a book of letters with Charles Bukowski, *Tough Company*. He is an established painter represented by Yard Dog Folk Art in Austin, Rainbow Man in Santa Fe and Liss Gallery in Toronto. A book of his art, *Blue Horse/Red Desert*, was published by Bangtail Press in 2011.

James Sallis has published sixteen novels including the Lew Griffin series, *Death Will Have Your Eyes, The Killer Is Dying* and *Drive*, from which the Cannes-winning film derived, plus multiple collections of stories, poems and essays, the standard biography of African-American writer Chester Himes, three books of musicology, and a translation of

Raymond Queneau's novel *Saint Glinglin*. He's also worked widely as critic and reviewer, and has received a lifetime achievement award from Bouchercon, the Hammett Award for literary excellence in crime writing, and the Grand Prix de Littérature policière. Recent books include the novel *Others of My Kind* and *Black Night's Gonna Catch Me Here: New and Selected Poems*. A new novel, *Willnot*, is due in the spring 2016 from Bloomsbury.

Martín Solares was born in Mexico. He completed a doctorate at La Sorbonne and lives in Mexico City. He is also a director at Tusquets Editores México, and a member of the Sistema Nacional de Creadores de Arte. *The Black Minutes* was shortlisted for the Rómulo Gallego International Novel Prize and has been translated into numerous languages.

John Stickney lives, works and publishes poetry, fiction and prose from Cleveland, Ohio. His story appeared in slightly different form in *Thuglit*.

Made in the USA
Monee, IL
22 December 2019

19399127R00111